A Vineyard Christmas Guest

THE VINEYARD SUNSET SERIES

KATIE WINTERS

Chapter One

The baby on all fours smack-dab in the center of the Sheridan house living room knew precisely the power of manipulation he had over his elder Sheridans. There in his little mustard-yellow button-down and his diaper, he clambered forward, his ocean-blue eyes shining. His dark curls tickled across the upper edge of his ear, and his face erupted into a magnetic smile that was just as powerful as the bright sun. Only nine months before, Audrey had given birth to baby Max Wesley Sheridan, and since then, he'd grown like a bad weed and now weighed almost twenty pounds. He could even pull himself up to a standing position and had begun to babble out nonsensical words, proof he was almost brave enough to try out a real word of his own.

In every way, this once very sick baby at the NICU, Audrey's tiny miracle, had traveled through time with the rest of them, changing and growing so much stronger.

And Audrey felt she'd missed every second of it.

"He's coming to you, Momma," Lola announced in a bright tone as Max hobbled toward Audrey, smacking his palms against the carpet.

Audrey dropped onto her knees and brought her arms out wide. Her smile stretched her cheeks as Max buzzed his lips with excitement.

"Come on, Max. You can do it. Come to me," Audrey urged him on, just before she bent down and lifted him into her embrace. His once-soft and downy baby smell had shifted slightly. She stretched a hand behind his head and bobbed him against her as his large eyes widened. They held one another's gaze for a long moment, both captivated. She had only a couple of hours left before her mother planned to drive her back to Penn State for her final few weeks before Christmas break. Audrey planned to use every second she had.

"Can I get anyone a piece of pie?" Susan Sheridan Frampton stepped out from the kitchen, rubbing her hands against a red-checkered apron that had once belonged to Anna Sheridan, Audrey's grandmother.

"I'd love a piece, please. I guess I could put on a few more pounds." Christine laughed as she spread a hand over her large pregnant stomach.

"I can't believe we still have some," Lola stated now as she jumped up to help. "I figured we'd clear that out by Saturday, at least."

"We always over-prepare on pie," Susan affirmed. "Audrey? Amanda? You good for a slice?"

Audrey's cousin Amanda was wrapped up in a thick blanket across the living room, her pencil poised over a crossword puzzle.

She chewed distractedly at the edge and then hurriedly scribed whatever answer she'd just come up with across the page.

"Audrey?" Susan tried again without an answer from either of them.

"Oh, sure. I guess it wouldn't be the Sunday after Thanksgiving if I didn't stuff myself with leftovers until I regret every decision I've ever made." Audrey walked toward the kitchen with Max on her hip, bobbing him as he buzzed and popped his lips.

"I received a few more photos from Aunt Kerry." Lola slid her phone from her pocket and flashed it toward Susan and her daughter as Susan sliced a knife through the center of a pecan pie. In the image, Susan and Lola's younger cousin, Andy, kissed his new bride, Beth, in the backyard of Trevor and Kerry Montgomery's home. The spontaneous marriage had occurred the previous afternoon after a volatile and confusing engagement.

"She's wearing Grandma Marilyn's dress?" Susan all-but shrieked yet managed to cling to the knife with white fingers.

"I guess they dragged it out of the attic and realized it fit Beth like a glove," Lola affirmed as her eyebrows rose.

"I didn't know that was an option." Susan muttered distractedly, her voice edged with a little jealousy.

"Come on, Susan. You looked like a dream at your wedding," Lola told her. "And you know how difficult it was for Beth and Andy to come together— with Andy being overseas for so long, and Beth all alone with her baby... Gosh, when I think of it..." She pressed her hand over her heart as her eyes grew shadowed.

"Of course. Of course." Susan shook her head distractedly as she slid several slabs of apple, pumpkin, and pecan pie onto small china plates. "Apple?" She glanced at Audrey and then warmed her face at Max's babbling.

"Pumpkin, I think," Audrey replied.

Susan slid the plate across her palm and dotted a fork to the left of the orange triangular slab of goodness. Since Audrey's arrival Wednesday afternoon, she hadn't gone more than an hour or two without eating something that was stuffed full of carbs and overloaded with sugar— and her stomach gurgled with borderline aggression.

"Audrey, I feel like I hardly got a chance to sit with you these past few days," Susan admitted. "Our lives here on the Vineyard have been so chaotic; it's so beautiful to imagine you out there, working tirelessly to pursue your dreams. I know Max will be so proud of this story when he's old enough to understand. I feel that's one of the greatest things I did for my children— reach for what I wanted. Finish my law degree. Practice to the best of my ability, despite dance recitals and chicken pox and all the things life throws at you as a parent."

Audrey's stomach tightened with sorrow. How could she illustrate how difficult the previous few months had been for her? With only a few hours left before her return, she couldn't just vomit out the darkness in her heart, which had only grown denser over the previous semester.

"Oh, it's been busy," Audrey said, her voice overly bright and false.

"I'm sure," Susan offered. She then passed through the kitchen doorway to deliver slabs of pie to Christine and Amanda, who initially refused before placing it on the little side table beside her. Probably, she'd pick at it for the next three hours.

Audrey's mother Lola's eyes seemed all-seeing. She leaned against the furthest kitchen counter and crossed arms against her chest. "Do you have a lot of papers to write before the end of the semester?"

"It feels like a never-ending stream of papers," Audrey affirmed.

"I'm sure. Have you signed up for your next semester of classes?" Lola asked.

Audrey's heart jumped into her throat, just as the back door that led from the driveway, through the mudroom, and then into the vibrant warmth of the living room, kitchen, and dining area, creaked open, bringing with it a crisp rush of late-November air. Grandpa Wes hollered excitedly in greeting.

"We saw him!"

Audrey hunkered back from her mother's question and grinned up at one of her favorite people in the world, a man who'd provided a backbone of support for her over the previous year and a half since her discovery of her pregnancy, her nine months of ballooning, and then her devastating weeks of being a new mother to a baby latched away in the NICU. Despite his dementia diagnosis, Grandpa Wes was frequently a sharp-edged character, an avid bird-watcher, and wickedly funny, apt to hurl silly insults and sarcastic remarks just as quickly as Audrey could dish them back.

"The big cardinal again?" Audrey asked.

Kellan, Scott's teenage son, who'd recently built up a profound friendship with his step-grandfather, stepped around Grandpa Wes, grabbed a plate of apple pie from Susan's outstretched hand, thanked her, and then beamed up at Wes.

"It's like the cardinal just knows when Wes will be out there," Kellan affirmed. "I look for him on my own, and he stays away."

Wes puffed out his chest proudly. He then removed his fingers

5

from his gloves and wrapped his first finger and thumb around Max's meaty palm as Max cooed with excitement.

"That's right, Max. I saw him again. You and Christine saw him with me a few weeks ago, remember? You pointed up at him and said, 'Ga!'"

Christine burst into laughter, so much so that her pie plate nearly dropped from her pregnant belly.

"Audrey, you should have seen Max," Christine offered. "The bird landed on a tree branch only about as tall as Dad's head. Max's eyes were about as big as saucers."

"I think we're raising ourselves a future bird watcher," Grandpa Wes said brightly.

Audrey's throat tightened. Here it was: the hundredth memory her family had of her baby during the months she'd been away. What had she done during that time? Her memories revolved around her frequent drives from Penn State to Martha's Vineyard and back again, as those hours were charged with a supersonic level of guilt and emotion. Everything else seemed a stream of burnt coffee, overcharged at the library, horrific flirtations from fraternity brothers, papers turned in two to three minutes prior to their due time, and stress so bad it made her want to vomit.

There was a rap at the back door. Kellan marched around Wes, as though he owned the place these days and yanked open the door. A familiar voice swirled out from behind the whoosh of the wind.

"Hi! Is Audrey here?"

Fearful and unwilling to look at anything else, Audrey turned her large eyes back toward Max, whose eyelids had begun to curl downward. Her heart shattered. This would be the last time she put him to sleep before she had to return to school.

"She's right here, actually!" Kellan had been so resistant to the Sheridan family, yet now found himself overjoyed at his inclusion, it seemed. Audrey currently resented it.

Nine months before, when Audrey had spent her long, gut-wrenching days at the NICU, she'd met a young man named Noah. Noah's mother had given birth to a sick baby, and he'd walked the halls of the hospital, grabbing meals for his mother, tending to loose ends, all in expectation of his sister's release. They'd met at a vending machine, which now in hindsight seemed so silly, during a time when Audrey's devastation had been so complete that she almost hadn't been able to form words with her own tongue.

In Noah's words, at the end of the summer, he'd fallen "head over heels" for Audrey.

Audrey's feelings had matched his. But that had been in August. And currently, her heart was shattered— she had four papers due, and the concept of romance felt as distant as the planet of Neptune. When she looked at herself in the mirror, she no longer saw the glamorous beauty she'd felt herself to be (especially around the time when her older colleague at her Chicago-based internship had gotten her pregnant).

His texts had been frequent; his calls had come three or four times a week. His masculine baritone voice had calmed her and excited her for the first few weeks of the semester. Once a wave of depression had crashed over her, the voice had become a nagging reminder of how small and unworthy of love she truly felt.

"Happy Thanksgiving!" Noah held a bouquet of flowers and beamed down at her as he entered the kitchen.

"Noah! It's good to see you." Lola, ever sociable, pressed a hand across Noah's upper arm in greeting. "I thought you'd be here a bit earlier this weekend, but I guess you had a number of family obligations."

Noah blinked at Audrey expectantly. He'd asked her precisely seven times if he could stop by the Sunrise Cove Inn on Thanksgiving Day to meet her extended family. Instead of texting him back, she had burrowed her face in Max's luscious hair and left the text unanswered.

"I guess you're about to head out," Noah said. To his credit, his voice held no resentment.

"Looks like it." Audrey shifted Max against her as his head grew heavier with sleep.

"Why don't you two head out to the porch?" Lola suggested. "I can take Max."

"No. I have him." Audrey's tone was sharp-edged. There was no taking it back, now.

Audrey left her untouched slice of pie on the counter and led Noah toward the enclosed back porch, with its glittering view of the Vineyard Sound beyond. The Vineyard Sound at the end of November was a far different beast than the glorious, turquoise waters of mid-June or July. It was grey and tumultuous and unforgiving.

"It's good to see you," Noah said after she'd pushed the porch door shut.

"You too."

Months before, when the house had been mostly empty, and Grandpa Wes had latched himself away for the night, she and Noah had cuddled on this very porch, peering out at the twinkling stars that ignited so brightly against the immensity of the night.

She could never have envisioned the sight of him would make her stomach flip upside down.

Silence seemed monstrous, but Audrey felt unwilling to bridge the divide between herself and this relative stranger.

"You have a couple more weeks left?" he asked.

"That's what they tell me." Audrey very well could have thrown up right there across the porch.

"I hope we get to see each other a little bit more over your Christmas break," Noah told her. "It's been really boring on this island without you."

Audrey's nostrils flared. There was nothing worse than having someone in love with you when you weren't sure how to love yourself. Max's lips shivered open into a yawn, which surprised him. He awakened totally and let out a wild yelp.

"Shhh." Audrey cupped Max's head to try to calm him. In truth, she didn't have the same skills with him that she'd developed over the summer. He wasn't as accustomed to her as he was to Christine, who now raised him, or Lola, who often took him off Christine for nights at a time.

"He's getting so big," Noah observed, trying to side-step his previous sentiment.

But Audrey's eyes snapped up toward his. He stopped short as his smile fell from his face. Max's wails continued. They were a kind of soundtrack to the rift that now existed between them.

"I just don't know if I can do this anymore, Noah. I'm so busy with school and with Max."

"I know that you're busy. But I'm willing to do whatever I can to..."

"Well, maybe you shouldn't be willing," Audrey blared then. "You'd be much better with someone with less on her mind, that's for sure. I can't be funny or interesting or whatever it is you need. I can hardly be myself right now. Do you understand?"

Noah's cheeks sagged. He looked like a greyhound dog that knew his running career was over. He opened his lips to speak, just as Susan pressed open the back door and said, "Hey Noah! Can I get you a slice of pie? It turns out we made enough pie to feed a small village."

This was the Susan way. She was the eternal mother goose. Audrey resented it just then.

"I'm good, Susan," Noah hollered back. "I have to get back to my own family soon. We've got leftovers of our own to eat."

Noah then made intense eye contact with Audrey before he again bucked through the porch door and headed into the warmth of the Sheridan family. As though someone had pressed the laugh-track button, they all burst into laughter at something someone had said. Max wailed against Audrey's chest as her own heart burst with fear and sorrow.

At this moment out on the back porch, her eyes toward the ballooning moon on the horizon, Audrey felt she'd made every mistake possible.

Chapter Two

It was about a week and a half after Thanksgiving, and Christine and Zachery had neglected their Christmas decorating, swapping it for what Christine termed "moderate levels of constant baby-panic."

Now, after a wayward and very, very slow journey through the Oak Bluffs Christmas Tree Farm, they'd arrived home to fling Christmas cheer all over the house. Zach staggered forward, his arms filled with the long-limbed, shaggy green Christmas tree. He positioned it firmly in the corner of the living room, five feet to the left of the fireplace and directly beside the old black and white photograph Christine had recently hung of her mother, Anna. In the photo (which they'd discovered in the attic of the Sheridan house), Anna was pregnant with one of her daughters, her eyelashes fluttering across her cheeks and the sunlight blisteringly bright across her hair. Sometimes, looking at the photograph felt like a knife straight through the heart. But with her own pregnancy a constant, Christine felt she needed her mother there, guiding her in this small yet consequential way.

With the Christmas tree positioned, Zach jumped back and splayed a handout. "Ta-da!"

Christine scrunched her nose. "Lola? Can you come out here and get a read on this?"

Lola, who'd arrived with Max ten minutes after their return from the Christmas Tree Farm, stepped in from the kitchen with Max against her chest and a bottle poised near his lips. "Oh. I see..."

"What?" Zach was exasperated.

"Yeah. It's not going to work there," Christine affirmed.

Zach smacked his thighs and turned his face toward the fireplace, muttering inwardly.

"You got something you'd like to say, Zachery?" Lola teased.

"Oh, nothing. Just that that's the third place, we've tried for the Christmas tree in the past, oh, twenty-five minutes? And none of them have worked for you. You're both impossible."

Christine and Lola exchanged glances as Max smacked his palms together happily.

"Let's just put it on the roof, for goodness sake," Zachery tried.

Lola tossed her head back with laughter. "Maybe you can ask Santa and his reindeer to help you with that."

"Good one, Lola," Zach returned, rolling his eyes.

"Let's leave it there for now," Christine offered finally.

Lola shrugged. "It's already December 8th, you know. You'd better make your Christmas decorating decisions now. Plus, there's a possibility the baby will come early, and you'll have these Christmas decorations up until April."

"Thanks for the reminder that everything we know about life is about to fall apart," Christine returned sarcastically.

"Always here for you, big sis."

Christine stood and waddled toward the kitchen to check on the Christmas cookies she had slipped into the oven several minutes before. The reindeer- and bell- and holly-shaped cookies swelled upward expectantly. Lola disappeared to put Max in his crib and then reappeared to pour herself a glass of wine.

"You want one, Zach?"

"After the pain and turmoil you two just put me through?" he called back.

"I take it you want one?" Lola teased.

"Yes, Lola. I want one." Zach's disgruntled tone made both Christine and Lola shiver with laughter.

Christine poured herself a mug of tea and eased into the kitchen chair nearest the window. Lola sipped her wine contemplatively as Christmas tunes rang out of the radio, one that Zach had reported purchasing in the year 2002.

"How's our girl doing?" Christine asked softly. Her correspondence with Audrey had whittled down to photos of Max, almost exclusively. Christine and Audrey's once-vibrant aunt-niece relationship no longer seemed as powerful.

"Oh, gosh. She seems a bit off to me." Lola curled her lips together and blinked out the window.

"I thought that at Thanksgiving," Christine offered. "Maybe she's burning the candle at both ends. She may be spreading herself too thin."

"I think it's a necessary part of life, being twenty and burning yourself out," Lola breathed. "But I can't pretend to know what it's like to be a young mother without her baby. I brought Audrey with me everywhere. She was a necessary weight of my everyday existence. I sometimes wonder if this separation from Max is self-inflicted harm, you know."

Christine's lips curved down as she fell beneath the heaviness of these words. "But she's much too stubborn to be told what to do."

"And if I was her age, I wouldn't want any kind of advice either," Lola affirmed. "We promised her we would care for her baby while she fought for her professional career."

Christine's voice cracked as she spoke. "And helping raise him with you and Susan and Amanda has genuinely been one of the greatest joys of my life. It's allowed Zach and I a trial run before we bring another baby into the world."

"I got it!" Zach appeared in the kitchen doorway with a boyish grin smeared across his face. He helped Christine to her feet and led her back into the living room, where he had positioned the Christmas tree to the right of the fireplace, alongside the glow of the vintage lamp and with a sterling view through the bay window from the street.

Christine's heart swelled. Deep within her, her baby stretched a foot against her insides, seemingly in agreement.

"It's perfect," she breathed. She didn't need Lola's eyes on it to know how true this was. She linked her fingers with Zach's as her eyes widened with a mixture of sorrow and excitement. The sorrow, she supposed, was linked to the fact that they would never get to do precisely this again. This, their first Christmas so tightly linked; this, their first Christmas before their first baby. It could only happen once. She prayed to soak up every second of the joy she was feeling.

With the Christmas cookies out of the oven, Lola scrubbed the baking sheet while Christine watched the snowflakes flutter outside the window.

"It should be perfect," Lola said. "Tommy's away for most of January, which means I'll just hang out at the Sheridan house with little Max-y while you and Zach and baby Walters get all cozied up in here. No reason you should destroy yourself with two babies when I have these two hands... plus a very-capable Amanda and Susan duo who can take the reins at will."

Christine laughed as her baby did somersaults inside her belly yet again. "What is it they say? It takes a village to raise a child?"

"They say it for a reason," Lola affirmed.

A few minutes later, Susan called to report that she, Amanda, and Kellan were in the midst of decorating the tree at the Sheridan house. "We have eggnog and hot cider and hot mulled wine," Susan announced through the speaker. "And never enough people around to drink it all."

Zach, Christine, Lola, and Max piled into Zachery's minivan, a recent purchase in the wake of Christine's pregnancy and their decision to take on Max till Audrey's arrival back to the island. Christine teased him from the backseat with Lola and Max, saying, "Look at you. You're all set and ready to become a soccer dad."

"Not for a few more years. And you know that I would never bring a soccer kid into this world. We're a baseball family," Zach affirmed as he eased the vehicle a bit too slowly down the snow-glossed roads.

"Whatever you say, Daddio," Christine replied with a laugh.

The Sheridan house was in a state of Christmas flux. Scott had purchased the Christmas tree from the same Christmas Tree Farm on December 1st, but Susan and Amanda had been up to their ears in legal clients as of late, and Grandpa Wes hadn't had the physical or mental strength to decorate the tree on his own. "That and it's not like I have an artistic eye," he'd told them over dinner a few days before.

"Where's Dad?" Christine asked as she eased through the door belly-first.

"He's at Aunt Kerry's," Susan announced as she furrowed her brow, on the hunt for the perfect position for a Christmas bulb.

"We thought we'd surprise him," Amanda said as she bounced up on her toes to position the angel at the top of the tree.

"It's a relief to be somewhere other than our own Christmas mess," Zach said as he shifted into the kitchen to pour himself a glass of mulled wine.

"That's kind of why we left our place, right Kellan?" Susan stated with a mischievous smile.

"The Christmas tree that Dad picked out for our place is... interesting, to say the least," Kellan affirmed.

"What does that mean?" Lola asked with an eyebrow cocked.

"It's like in *Christmas Vacation*," Susan started to explain as she scrunched her nose. "I love the man to death, but he really Clark Griswald-ed this one."

"Too big?" Christine asked.

"Enormous," Susan responded, her eyes wide as saucers.

"You basically can't sit in the living room right now," Kellan affirmed. "I've thought about taking Grandpa Wes over there to bird watch. I'm sure there's something flying around in there."

Lola erupted with laughter and collapsed on the couch to hunt through the box of Christmas decorations. Amanda grinned wildly and greeted her Aunt Christine with a kiss on her cheek. She looked half-drunken and giggly. She soon leaned toward Christine's ear and whispered, "Sam's coming by after his shift."

The previous year had been a whirlwind for Amanda. She had begun January as a blushing fiancé, with plans to marry her long-time boyfriend, Chris. By the end of January, Chris left her at the altar, and Amanda was left to stare into the abyss that had opened in the wake of his departure. These days, Chris gallivanted around Asia while Amanda teetered into another relationship with the newly-hired Sunrise Cove Inn manager, Sam. She'd never confirmed anything to her aunts nor to her mother— yet they'd seen the way the two twenty-somethings looked at one another. Their glances sizzled with love and expectation.

"That's incredible, Amanda," Christine murmured, her heart swelling with love. "You deserve all the happiness in the world. I hope you know that."

"Who wants a buckeye?" This was Susan, who stepped out of the kitchen with a platter of peanut butter and chocolate Christmas delights. She bent low to allow Christine to grab one from her collapsed state on the chair nearest the Christmas tree.

Christine pressed her teeth through the melted chocolate and dug into the gooey peanut butter beneath. A moan escaped her lips. With her eyes closed, surrounded with laughter and conversation and countless familiar smells— there in the Sheridan house of all places— Christine found it very easy to convince herself that actually, she was eleven years old, and Anna Sheridan had prepared this buckeye, instead.

Christmas was a time of gut-wrenching nostalgia, of new memories morphing with the old. It was, therefore, a near-perfect time to bring a new baby into the world. Her baby would be shrouded with the love of many decades of time passed away.

Zach's phone buzzed a moment later as he lifted a Christmas ornament to the tree.

"You are not going into the Bistro yet, Mister," Christine told him firmly.

Zach shook his head. "It's not the Bistro." He then snapped the phone to his ear and asked, "Joshua. What's going on?"

Slowly, Zach's face transitioned from friendly confusion to one of fear and panic.

"What's he saying?" Zach demanded as he walked back toward the mudroom, apparently to get his shoes.

Christine, Susan, and Lola exchanged glances. Zach reappeared in the hallway and beckoned for them to follow.

"We'll be right there, Joshua. Thank you for letting me know as soon as possible."

Zach dropped his phone into his coat pocket and then flung it around his shoulders. His voice was hard-edged and strange.

"My friend who works on the ferry just found Wes up around the docks, wandering around. He seems confused," he told them.

"What are you talking about?" Kellan jumped up, nearly spilling his hot cocoa.

"Let's go..." Susan cried as she reached for her own coat.

Christine, Lola, and Amanda were hot on Susan's heels. After a scrambled reach for coats and boots and hats, Lola cried, "I can't believe this. I'll stay here with the baby while you all go."

"No use in all of us going," Amanda agreed. "Kellan? Let's stay put."

Kellan grumbled inwardly as the color drained from his cheeks.

"I'm coming with you," Susan told Christine and Zach with finality.

There she was again: their mother hen, Susan Sheridan. But Christine wanted the weight of her support. She nodded firmly as she slipped her bright red hat over her head.

"Let's go."

Chapter Three

In the front seat, Susan spoke frantically with Aunt Kerry over the phone. Zach quickly drove them down the mud-puddle and snow-filled gravel driveway before he surged them out onto the main road. Christine had to remind herself to breathe as she clenched her fists on either side of her thighs. Each snowflake seemed overdone, nearly the size of quarters.

"He told you that he was up at the Sunrise Cove with me?" Susan blared to Aunt Kerry.

On the other end of the phone, Aunt Kerry's voice was panicked and strained. Christine couldn't make out her words. Her heart pumped with fear as she reckoned with what this meant. When Susan shoved her phone back into her coat pocket, she said, "Dad seemed to think he wanted to work at the Cove tonight while the rest of us 'hung out.'"

Christine grumbled inwardly as she spread her fingers out across her stomach. "He tricked us."

"He told me a few days ago that he feels better than he has in years," Zach explained with the flip of his hand.

"He got arrogant," Susan breathed. "That's so typical of Wes Sheridan, isn't it? Thinking he's too good for his diagnosis."

"Let's not jump to conclusions," Christine called from the backseat.

Susan whipped around in her seat to show the extreme volatility that stormed behind her eyes. "We've done our darnedest to keep him safe over the past year and a half. He's the entire reason we all came together on this island. We can't just lose him to the cold Martha's Vineyard winter due to his arrogance."

Christine snapped her lips together, amazed at the incredible weight of Susan's anger. Naturally, fear was the reason behind it: fear and a tremendous amount of love.

"Did he say what he was muttering about?" Susan demanded of Zach as she lurched back around.

"He said they couldn't understand him," Zach reported.

They pulled up alongside the ferry docks. Snow fluttered around them as they hustled toward the office nearest to the docks, where the dock workers sold tickets and passed out pamphlets to tourists. Susan lingered, trying to stay back to ensure Christine didn't waddle alone in the dark. Zach charged forward to greet Joshua, a sixty-something man who'd driven the ferries to Woods Hole and back again for decades, just like his father before him.

"Hey, Zach." Joshua shook Zach's hand firmly but gave no smile.

"We can't thank you enough," Zach flashed him a grateful smile. He gestured back toward Christine and Susan as they approached. "I brought a couple of the Sheridan Sisters to lure him home again."

"That should do it," Joshua replied. "Good evening to you both. I haven't seen you for quite some time."

Christine nodded firmly while Susan shot through the narrow, crooked doorway to find Wes. Christine hobbled up behind her and witnessed her eldest sister, stopping short before a hunched-over, tired, shivering and confused version of Wes Sheridan, who clutched a mug of hot coffee for dear life and muttered to himself. His eyes seemed unseeing and lost.

"Dad?" Susan murmured softly, not wanting to scare him.

Wes muttered a bit more, sometimes a bit louder, other times a bit softer; his voice was like a wave, crashing in on the shore and then dissipating.

"Hi, Dad." Christine slipped alongside him and placed a hand over his. He hardly registered it.

"I think we should bring him up to the hospital?" Zach suggested from the doorway.

"He wasn't out there that long," Joshua reported. "He walked over from the Sunrise Cove. No more than ten minutes, I guess. When I saw he looked confused, I sat him down in here to wait for you."

"We can't thank you enough," Christine tried, although her words seemed useless.

"Dad? What happened?" Susan muttered. She dropped to a crouch and peered up at him.

Finally, Wes was able to articulate a word that Christine could only make half-sense of.

"Willa... Where is Willa?" Wes licked his chapped lips expectantly as he turned his eyes back toward Christine. "Willa?"

Christine's jaw dropped. She and Susan shared a moment of sincere shock.

"Willa? You mean Aunt Willa?" Susan demanded.

"Willa. Of course. Willa." Wes seemed half-excited, half-confused. He sipped his coffee as his eyes sparkled. "Willa."

"Let's get him home," Susan breathed. "Maybe once he warms up and gets some sleep, he'll be able to explain himself." She stood and turned back to face Zach. "Will you help me walk him out to the van?"

Once in the van, Christine sat next to her father in the back-seat, with Max's car seat there between them. She placed her hand over his yet again and felt her warmth as a great contrast to his continued chill.

"Beautiful snowfall tonight," Wes informed them primly as they drove back to the Sheridan house in relief.

Susan dropped her head with a firm thud against the back of her seat. Exasperation didn't cover it.

When Zach parked in the driveway, Lola flew out of the back door and hustled for the van. She opened Wes's door and gazed at him lovingly, but also fearfully.

Wes lifted his chin to greet his youngest daughter warmly. "There she is. Willa. It's been so long, hasn't it?"

Lola's eyes widened as the weight of this moment washed over her. "Let's get you inside, Dad. It's warm in there. Amanda's got Max all riled up. He's about to crawl up and down the walls." Her voice wavered as she unlatched Wes's seatbelt and helped him step out onto the gravel driveway.

Zach opened Christine's door and assisted her to the house. Exhaustion from the previous hour's events, plus the addition of about thirty pounds on her otherwise small frame, made Christine's ankles waver beneath her. Zach caught her elbow and muttered, "You okay?" while Lola and Wes stepped into the mudroom.

They stacked their boots in the corner as Amanda hustled into the doorway with Max on her chest. Her smile was full of confusion and she was clearly overwhelmed.

"Hi Grandpa," she said brightly as she stepped back to allow him to enter.

Soon after, he collapsed on his favorite, dark blue chair, the one with the picture-perfect view of the Vineyard Sound beyond. Zach admitted he had to head up to the Bistro to take inventory, an event that had to happen "one of these nights." He kissed Christine on the cheek and whispered, "Keep me updated on everything. I'm just a few minutes away." Everything seemed permeated with dread.

Christine joined her father as he looked out the window, splaying her hand across her belly and watching his contemplative face. During these soft, strange moments, Wes looked far older than his seventy-one years. Christine could half-envision them ten years from then— Wes at eighty-one instead. God willing, her baby would be nearly ten by then. God willing, they would still have so much of the goodness they had now.

But so much changed in a blink of an eye. She knew that. It was the only inevitable thing.

From where she sat, she could hear Susan and Lola muttering together in the kitchen about Wes's confusion.

"He won't stop talking about Willa?" Lola murmured.

"It's strange. Mom hardly mentioned her at all," Susan said. "And only mentioned her parents a few times. Mostly, I think, she worried that Dad was too much like her father when he drank."

Often, Susan operated as the authority of what Anna Sheridan did and did not do, as she'd been seventeen and the eldest at the time of her death. Christine knew that Lola resented this, especially as Lola had only been eleven at the time. She'd missed out.

Still, Lola seemed to dismiss her own feelings. "Yeah, I think Dad told me once they were big drinkers. Alcoholics, even— and abusive."

Christine lifted her chin to try to catch her father's eye. Lola appeared to give him a mug of tea, which he thanked her for before turning back toward the window. Lola shifted her weight anxiously.

"Dad? Can you hear me?" Lola tried.

Wes turned his head toward his youngest daughter. His smile illuminated the rest of his face.

"Lola! There you are."

The switch happened in an instant, as though he'd just been asleep and now erupted back into real-life. Christine's eyes were lined with tears. The abrupt switch was almost too much to bear.

"Are you feeling okay, Dad?" Lola asked in a soft, soothing voice.

"Right as rain," Wes told her.

"Dad... Were you working up at the Sunrise Cove tonight on your own?" Christine asked timidly.

Wes's eyes grew clouded. "Not on my own, no. That boy Sam was up there with me. Good man." He then directed his eyes toward Amanda, who still bobbed Max near the entrance to the staircase. "You could do much worse than that young man. I'll tell you that."

Amanda's cheeks blushed crimson as Christine stirred with confusion. Often, this was the way with Wes's dementia. He had good moments, bad moments, in-between moments— yet this Willa situation seemed like an outlier.

"Joshua found you up at the ferry docks." Susan stepped out of the kitchen with an accusatory, lawyer-like tone. "You were muttering something about Willa. Like you were looking for her..."

Wes's lips parted in surprise. "You mean your mother's little sister?"

Lola, Susan, and Christine exchanged worried glances. It was almost like he tried to gaslight them into the belief that what had happened actually hadn't.

"Why would you be up at the ferry docks looking for Aunt Willa, Dad?" Lola whispered, her voice cracking.

Wes grunted inwardly. He took another long sip of tea and wiped the back of his hand across his lips. He then stood slowly, his knees creaking beneath him, before ambling the rest of the way to his downstairs bedroom, which Scott had built for him off the side of the main house.

"I better hit the hay, girls," he told them. "I'll be brighter and better in the morning."

When the door clicked closed behind him, Lola dropped into the chair he'd vacated and smacked her palms over her cheeks. Her eyes glistened.

"It was like none of it happened at all," Susan murmured.

"I'm sure he'll have more to say about it tomorrow," Amanda tried. "Have any of you ever looked up your Aunt Willa at all?"

"Never..." Christine's throat tightened. "It's strange. We were always told Mom's family was a no-go, and we just sort of accepted that as fact."

Amanda's phone began to buzz in her pocket. Lola hustled

forward to bring a sleeping Max into her arms to allow Amanda to answer. Her smile curled toward her ears as she lifted her cell, proof that the caller on the other line was Sam.

"Hey there. I didn't think you were done until a bit later?"

Christine watched the many phases of Amanda's face over the following ten seconds. Her illumination and excitement soon gave way to confusion in the form of lowered eyebrows and parted lips. Her eyes then widened as shock took over before that same shock transformed into a look of disbelief.

"We'll be right there," Amanda breathed. "Thank you, Sam. I really meant it."

Slowly, she brought the phone from her ear and placed it tenderly at the center of her chest. Her eyes were the size of saucers. It was really like she'd just seen a ghost.

"Someone just entered the Sunrise Cove Inn," she explained firmly. "A mysterious guest named Willa McLavin. She says she's related to the Sheridan family— and she needs a room."

Chapter Four

"If you don't buckle your seatbelt, we'll never leave this driveway," Susan snapped at Lola in the front seat of her Prius. The seatbelt blinker had begun to blare annoyingly, like an always-nagging mother. It added an extra layer of stress to what already seemed like an evening straight from hell.

Lola grumbled inwardly as she drew the seatbelt across her lap and snapped herself in. She then flipped her long locks over her shoulder and eyed the orange light that beamed out from the Sheridan house window, where Amanda's shadow bobbed around as she struggled to put Max back to sleep.

"This is all so insane," Lola muttered finally.

"Do you think Dad knew about this all along, but got confused?" Christine asked.

Lola shrugged. "If he did, he conveniently let that part of his brain go, didn't he?"

"I'm sure he didn't do it on purpose," Christine countered, remembering how the older man had looked painfully exhausted mere moments before, so much so that she'd nearly traced through the reality of his impending death.

"I mean, this woman could be some kind of a drifter," Susan interjected as she eased the Prius through a whipping tunnel of snow. "She might have heard that Wes was all alone here on the island. Maybe she got a tip-off from someone that he had money. I mean, there's really no way we can know for sure that this woman is who she says she is."

"There she is. Superwoman Susan, to the rescue," Lola blurted.

Susan bristled. "If you'd seen the cases I've seen, you would be fearful, too."

This shut both Lola and Christine up for the duration of the ride up to the Sunrise Cove Inn, a place that Christine hadn't frequented for over a month, as it had grown far too painful to bake croissants from the wee hours of the morning as a balloon-shaped pregnant person. In truth, she'd missed it, missed the calm, dark quiet of those mornings alone as she stirred, mixed, kneaded, and baked herself into a flour-tinged oblivion. By the time of Zach's approximate nine o'clock arrival, she'd been eternally bright-eyed and bushy-tailed— ready to conquer a brand-new day, especially with Zach by her side.

The front desk now featured Sam and Natalie, the long-time middle-aged Sunrise Cove Inn hospitality worker, who'd shown tremendous allegiance to the Sheridan family over the years. Natalie's cheeks were white as paper. Sam hustled around the desk as he tapped his forehead with his handkerchief.

"Hi, Susan. Lola. Christine." He greeted them each with a personal nod. "I've set Willa up in the Bistro with a cup of tea."

"Thank you so much, Sam," Susan returned firmly.

"Did she say anything else?" Lola asked. "Besides being related to us?"

Sam's forehead stitched into wrinkles. "She seems kind of confused. Kind of like..." He stuttered slightly. "Kind of like people I've seen on drugs before if that makes any sense."

Susan's eyes widened with surprise. "Drugs?" she hissed.

"It's difficult to say. But only a few minutes ago, she stormed up to the desk and told me that the owner's wife is her sister, Anna. She keeps asking where Anna is. I wasn't sure what to say. I wasn't going to come out with, 'I'm pretty sure Anna died over twenty years ago,' because it's not really my business. So I just told her that the Sheridan family owns the Sunrise Cove Inn and that her family is on their way to pick her up. That settled her, at least for now."

Susan, Lola, and Christine formed a circle in the hallway between the Bistro and the Sunrise Cove Inn foyer and bent their heads low.

"Do you think she's really on drugs?" Lola whispered.

Susan shrugged. "As I said, we don't even know if this woman is really who she says she is. It all could be some kind of act."

"I just wish we knew more about this person." Christine closed her eyes somberly. "There's no telling what happened to her after she left the island with our grandparents."

They held the silence for a moment. The entrance of the Bistro seemed like a portal to some other world, one they weren't entirely sure they wanted to enter. Just then, Zach popped out of the Bistro kitchen and waved a sturdy hand.

"What are you three doing here?" he asked. "Want me to make you up a plate?"

"No thanks, babe," Christine called. She then took it upon

31

herself to take the first staggering step forward toward whatever "doom" this would bring. It was better to know reality than to run away from it. This was something Christine had had to learn over a number of chaotic years.

Zach continued toward Christine, as though she operated as a magnet. They met steps into the front of the Bistro, where Christine could peer out across the tables of flickering candlelight. Toward the far corner sat a woman in her early sixties, maybe, her hair a luscious dark brown just like the other Sheridan women, her dress a dark plum, sophisticated, as though she'd planned to dress up that night. A cup of tea steamed in front of her, seemingly untouched as she tapped the tips of her fingers across the table.

"Have you had any contact with that older woman in the corner?" Christine asked Zach.

"She told me she didn't want to eat anything," Zach said with a shrug. "That's all I know."

"Apparently, that's my Aunt Willa." Christine murmured.

"We don't know anything yet," Susan countered.

"So, Wes was actually up at the docks looking for her?" Zach ran his hands over his apron distractedly. "And you've never met her?"

"No. Susan seems to think she's some kind of a drifter," Lola whispered. "What do you think, Zach? Think that old woman will take everything we own?"

"Shhh," Susan hissed.

"I don't know if we should barge over to her table all at once," Christine murmured. "It would probably be overwhelming for her."

But just then, Susan made her way through the tables, past the old islander married couple who frequently dined at the Sunrise

Cove Bistro, past a couple with a young boy, around the age of six, who read his book at the table, his lips forming the words soundlessly. Christine wondered if Aunt Willa (if this really was their Aunt Willa) normally spent dinners like this alone; perhaps she had the near-constant view of other people's love and other people's family.

Christine realized, with a funny jolt in her stomach, that this image of their "Aunt Willa" was precisely how she'd envisioned her own life prior to her return to the Vineyard. How funny.

And how grateful she was that things hadn't turned out that way.

On cue, her baby stretched its foot against the outer ridge of her belly. Christine placed a tender hand over her stomach, lifted her chin, and followed after Susan. Lola was hot on her heels.

Once at the table, they found the woman with her neck bent forward and her hands flat against the top of the table. Susan scrunched up her face with fear. It seemed she'd come confidently to the table and promptly lost her courage.

"Willa?" Christine found a raspy, unconfident voice within her.

Slowly, the woman curved her neck back upright and blinked up toward the three Sheridan Sisters. Immediately, all three jaws of the Sheridan Sisters dropped to the floor.

This woman before them couldn't have been anyone but Anna Sheridan's younger sister. Every feature could have been pointed to directly upon the faces of the three sisters, down to the curve of Susan's nose and the wide yet beautiful eyes of Lola to the smaller, more precise features upon Christine's doll-like face.

And, of course, the view of this woman at age sixty sent a shiver up Christine's spine. It was as though they witnessed what their mother might have become had she not drowned that fateful night years before.

"Anna. You're here." Willa's eyes widened to match Lola's as she took in the full view of this gorgeous creature, Anna's near-twin. She lifted a wrinkled hand toward Lola's, and Lola pressed her fingers through hers as tears lined her eyes.

"It's not Anna," Lola breathed as she sat across from the older woman, her fingers still linked.

"Where do you live, Willa? Where did you come from?" Susan asked, ready to finalize the facts around the situation that was unfolding, while Lola wanted to remain in the emotion of it all.

But Willa's eyes remained upon Lola. Lola pressed her lips together as silence folded over them. You could have sliced the intensity of the air with a knife.

"You must have heard that we lost our mother, Anna, many years ago," Lola finally whispered.

Willa's face erupted with shock. She splayed her free hand across the porcelain of her cheek. "Of course. Of course. I remember now…" She closed her eyes tenderly and unlinked her fingers from Lola's. "I am terribly sorry. I sometimes…" She gestured around her skull, as though she alluded to a sort of mental diagnosis. "Sometimes I just… Go away."

Susan walked around to sit at the chair opposite Christine, which led Christine to collapse in this chair, as well. There they sat: Anna Sheridan's three daughters alongside the aunt they'd never known. They looked at one another with heavy curiosity and disbelief.

"Why are you here, Willa?" Christine whispered finally.

Willa's eyes welled with tears. She closed them again and pressed her fingers against her temples, drawing enormous circles against her skull. "Gosh, it just gets so chaotic in there... I can feel it. Like a storm."

Lola and Christine exchanged worried glances.

"Did you speak with our father about coming here tonight?" Susan asked.

"Who?" Willa's eyes popped back open as she tried to understand the question.

"Our father, Wes Sheridan. He was up at the docks looking for you," Susan explained.

Willa shook her head, incredulous.

"Your sister, Anna, married a man named Wes Sheridan," Lola tried, her voice tender. "You must have been around back then."

"Oh yes..." Willa's forehead became an accordion as she considered Lola's words. "Wesley. Anna was so smitten with him. I sat in her little room at our parents' house while she practiced what to say to him in the hallways at her high school. Gosh, I couldn't wait to go to that high school. I wanted to be just like Anna. But I was only ten years old... Lipstick and boys and even lockers seemed like this whole other life to me."

Lola giggled tenderly, which made Susan cast a strange look. Maybe this wasn't the time for such reminiscing. It was clear that there was something incredibly off with this woman— clear that she either wanted to be or had to be cagey about the story that had led her here. Christine wasn't sure they would get any sort of response out of her, not anything that would be of use to them, anyway.

Susan excused herself for a moment. Christine and Lola exchanged wordless glances before Willa turned her eyes toward Christine's stomach and said, "My goodness. You're about ready, aren't you?"

Christine laughed outright. Despite the murkiness of this situation, her pregnancy and impending childbirth seemed a very sure thing.

"That's what they tell me," she replied.

Willa's face darkened. "I could hardly believe when Anna went through with it. She'd always said she wouldn't. Our mother was no mother at all. And Anna worried... Well. She worried she would be just like her."

Susan reappeared at the corner of the table as Christine and Lola turned over Willa's strange confession. Anna hadn't envisioned herself to be a mother? That didn't align with any of Christine's memories around Anna Sheridan. She'd always seemed a portrait of love and laughter; she'd always offered brilliant playtime ideas and sewed them little dresses and taught them to swim. Yes, in truth, she'd cheated on Wes, which had resulted in her untimely death— but that affair hadn't had anything to do with motherhood. Or had it?

Was it possible that Anna's decision to have an affair was linked to her strained relationship with her parents and sister? Christine was no therapist, but she did feel as though they had just uncovered a mountain of pain within their mother's life. Why hadn't they known about this previously?

"Unfortunately, Willa, there isn't an extra room here at the Sunrise Cove Inn," Susan told her gently.

Willa's lips curved downward in devastation. "Isn't that just the way?"

"But..." Lola curved her eyes toward Susan, pleading.

Susan's eyes widened. She flipped her hands over so that her palms curved toward the sky.

"But we could probably offer you space in our home," Susan said finally. "I just have to check with my husband."

Susan disappeared to call Scott as Willa muttered to herself. Her eyes glazed over yet again, reminiscent, as Sam had said, of someone on drugs. Lola muttered into Christine's ear, "As if Susan has ever had to ask Scott about anything."

When Susan returned to the table, she announced that everything was all-set and ready for Willa's arrival. She assisted the shivering Willa to her feet as Christine walked toward the steamy kitchen to explain to Zach what they knew so far. He listened with furrowed brows, then asked, "Are you sure you should get yourself involved in all this drama so soon before the baby comes?"

Toward the back of the kitchen, one of their favorite servers-turned-kitchen-staff-member had accidentally dropped a large silver platter. It clanked across the floor; the sound echoed from wall to wall as Christine splayed her hands over her ears in response to the loud noise.

"I'll be fine," Christine assured Zach. "Just make sure you keep your own stress levels in check."

"Me? Stressed?" Zach joked. "You know I'm always easy-breezy."

"Sure thing, cook." Christine lifted up on her toes to plant a kiss on his cheeks. "I love you."

"I love you, too."

Christine headed back to Susan's Prius to find Willa safely buckled into the back, her hands folded across her lap like a child. Christine heaved herself into the back as well, while Lola and Susan sat up front. Willa pressed her hand against the fog of the window as they eased back out onto the road.

"When was the last time you were on the Vineyard, Willa?" Christine asked softly.

"It's been about forty years," Willa breathed. "Susan was only three months old. Just a little, tiny, itty-bitty thing. I only saw her once. But I dreamed of her constantly after we left this big old rock."

Up front, Susan seemed on the verge of a sudden breakdown. Throughout the previous hours, she'd been nothing but practicality, basically declaring that they couldn't trust Willa with a ten-foot pole.

She'd very clearly changed her tune the moment Willa mentioned Susan as a tiny baby in Anna Sheridan's arms.

Chapter Five

An hour later, after Willa fell into a deep sleep in the dense shadows of Susan's guest room, Christine, Susan, Lola, and Amanda sat around the kitchen nook table to decompress the night's events. Here, in Susan's newly-designed kitchen, with its glorious view of the rocky coastline beyond and the waves that flipped and flirted against the rocks, clambering high to catch the glow of the earnest moon, they fell into stunned silence. It had very much felt as though Anna Sheridan sat within the Prius alongside them.

Willa seemed almost a direct message from a woman they hadn't seen in more than twenty-five years.

Susan lifted a shaking arm to pour three glasses of wine while Christine sat once again with a mug of steaming tea. Pregnancy was one of the greatest privileges of her life, a joy immeasurable in nearly every way. Even still, her tongue ached for just a single drop of wine.

As though she could read her mind, Lola interjected with,

"Soon, Christine. We promise you that." She then lifted her glass of wine and nodded toward Christine's stomach with excitement. "Guess we'll get two new family members this winter. Not just one."

"Gosh." Susan collapsed at the kitchen table and rubbed her temple. "When she said that stuff about me as a baby…"

"It's just crazy to me…" Amanda breathed.

"We should check the diaries," Lola suggested suddenly.

"I don't even know if my heart can take it," Susan murmured, looking down at her hands.

"I think we need to know as much as we can," Christine countered. "It's obvious there's something wrong with this woman— something that we can't possibly understand right now. Maybe a bit more insight into Mom and Willa's life together will help us put the pieces of this puzzle together."

Amanda leaped up and tip-toed up the staircase. Everyone knew that Susan had moved Anna's diaries to her new house, to be kept in a fireproof box on her antique bookshelf on the second floor. Amanda reappeared with the box and its thousands of perfectly drawn-out words, glorious poetry that told the story of a mystery woman's life.

"Maybe around the time Susan was born?" Christine suggested to her niece.

Amanda leafed through the diaries to find the appropriate year. Lola grabbed another and hunted, as well.

"This one seems to be from her teenage years." Lola glazed a finger over the words, tracing the lines. "It's just all about how obsessed with Dad she is… Oh! And something about a beautiful dress that Grandma Marilyn made for her for Christmas."

"Isn't that so sweet?" Susan muttered as she tried to wipe away her tear-stained cheeks.

"But nothing about her parents? Her sister?" Christine asked, her head cocked to the side, waiting for a response.

"Hmm. I mean, it stands to reason that she wouldn't write about something that was hurting her so much," Lola tried.

"Good point," Amanda returned. "She would have wanted to focus on the future she was building with Grandpa." But at that moment, her eyes grew wide as she cried, "Ah! I found something."

Amanda flipped the book around to trace a very small portion of the little diary so they could read it.

Mom tried to see Susan again, but it was pretty damn clear she'd drank a half-bottle of vodka before she drove herself to Wes and I's new home. I could smell it on her breath and I could see it in the way she wavered to and fro in the driveway before she got up the energy to come in. I told her there was no way she could meet Susan, not like this. She accused me of keeping her away from her granddaughter and accused me of excommunicating from our family.

The truth is, of course, that I haven't felt a part of that family in many years.

But she got nasty with me when I tried to close the door. She told me that there was no way I'd see Willa again if I didn't allow her to see Susan.

My heart aches for poor Willa, alone in that house. I haven't a clue what to do about it, especially with all the sleepless nights and the anxiety around new motherhood.

I can't imagine building a life for my children the way my mother has built ours. It was a miracle that I met Wes in the first place— a miracle that he loved me. I don't plan to mess that up.

"Oh my god," Lola breathed.

Susan placed her hands against her eyes as a wail escaped her. Amanda jumped up and wrapped her arms around her mother, holding her tightly as emotion rolled through her.

"It just makes me think of all my dark nights as a new mother," Susan explained as she tried to calm herself down. "Always thinking that you're doing everything wrong. Always wanting to build a better world. I can't think of a single night during those early days that I didn't really wish my mother was there beside me to help. And now, to hear that actually, our mother didn't have her mother, either." Susan then shifted her eyes toward her daughter's as her body shook. "I'm just so damn grateful right now that I made it through my bout of cancer."

"Mom..." Amanda seemed both alarmed and unsure about the sudden storm of emotions. She rubbed Susan's back as silence welled around them.

"We're pretty damn glad, too," Christine finally mustered.

Susan hiccupped and then burst into strange laughter. She tossed her head back so that her newly-grown locks cascaded down her shoulders.

"I just haven't thought about those dark nights of early motherhood in ages," Susan said.

Christine sighed longingly as she rubbed her stomach. Fear welled within her. Those nights were headed straight toward her.

"But you'll have us. Remember that," Lola pointed out, as though she could read Christine's mind.

"I think we should all get some serious sleep tonight," Amanda advised then, taking the reins just like her mother before her. "There are more diary entries to read and more conversations to be had with Willa. But right now? Right now, I think our bodies deserve to sleep." She then gave Lola a vibrant smile as she added, "And just a few days before Audrey's big return. I can't wait."

"Neither can I," Lola agreed. "I know she's studying hard for her finals. I hope she isn't driving herself crazy."

"I'm sure she's at-least half crazy," Amanda affirmed. "But that's all part of it. Probably, it's part of why she went back, to get swept up in it all again. To feel like a normal twenty-year-old again."

"I hope you're right," Lola murmured.

Christine longed to interject that there was no going back to being a "normal twenty-year-old" after giving birth. But she kept her lips pressed tightly closed in support of Amanda's suggestion. Sleep was a necessity. Perhaps tomorrow would allow greater understanding. She knew it always did.

Christine woke at the Sheridan house the following morning to a buzzing text message from Susan. When she twisted around to grab her phone, she caught sight of an old Alanis Morrissett poster, which she herself had hung on that very wall back in the nineties. It forced her mind through flashbacks of hundreds of other mornings— mornings when her limbs hadn't been so heavy, her stomach filled with so much ache. The baby pumped its foot against her stomach once more as Christine cooed, "Yeah, yeah. I know. You miss your daddy." Christine had all but hobbled through the thicket of trees last night between the Sheridan house and Susan's new place before ultimately falling into bed with her feet swelled and aching.

It was just like Susan to text before six in the morning.

SUSAN: Willa woke up around five-thirty. She seems confused. She's asking me more questions about where Anna is.

SUSAN: I think I want to take her to the emergency room. I have time before my afternoon appointments.

Christine groaned. Slowly, she shifted her heavy frame upright, so that her tip-toes danced across the upper part of the woven rug.

CHRISTINE: Just give me a few minutes to get dressed. Pick me up in the driveway?

Susan returned with a "thumbs up."

Christine donned a turtleneck, a thick dark blue sweater, a pair of maternity pants, and a puffy light green coat and blinked at herself in the downstairs hall mirror. If she had seen herself like this two years previously, when she'd been something of a fashion icon in New York City, she would have scoffed. "It's just you and me against that Martha's Vineyard winter cold," she whispered now, mostly to her baby but also to her reflection. "Nothing else matters, now."

Susan's Prius lights swelled through the morning haze. Christine waddled toward the backseat and then entered to hear a muttering, confused Willa, whom Susan had apparently lassoed up front. Susan had Lola on the phone, in which she was going to update her on their plans.

"I know you have Max," Susan said primly. "I just wanted to inform you of our plans. Maybe you could meet us back at the house in a few hours when we know more."

Lola seemed to respond groggily. Although Max was a relatively good all-night sleeper, it was possible that he'd picked the previous night to be finicky. Babies sensed the tension in the air. It could be said that they acted reasonably toward that tension. Christine often wanted to toss her head back and scream when panic set in.

Up at the hospital, Christine and Susan stood on either side of Willa and led her through the double-wide doors. The emergency waiting room was extremely illuminated, the sort of light that reminded Christine of cheap clothing stores' dressing rooms. You could see every flaw. The emergency room itself wasn't that busy, but the five people who sat within the waiting room were perhaps the most fatigued creatures on earth. The half-moon circles beneath their eyes told a story of having been awake all night long.

Susan checked Willa in as Christine and Willa found two plastic seats near the window. It was now six-fifteen, and the dim grey light of a winter's morning had begun to swell over the top of the glittering island snow.

"I just need to speak to her," Willa muttered under her breath as her eyes cut left and right. "I need her to know..."

As the emergency room wasn't entirely busy, a nurse named Camilla stepped out ten minutes later to take Willa back through the overly-bright halls. Susan and Christine followed behind but were left out of the examination room, as Camilla reported that she needed space with the patient alone to get a better read on her psychiatric health. Outside the door, Christine and Susan were wordless.

It was here, during Willa's check-up, at six-forty-five in the morning, that Christine felt the first tremendous jolt of pain. Her muscles tightened over her stomach as her knees buckled beneath her. She gasped and leaned back against the wall as Susan's eyes widened.

"What's wrong, Chris?" Susan demanded. "Are you having a contraction?"

"No, it's nothing," Christine told her as the pain subsided just as quickly as it had started.

"Are you sure?" Susan asked again, trying to read Christine's facial expression.

Christine blew the air out of her lips as she blinked herself back to full consciousness. "Yes, of course."

Just then, Camilla pushed open the door to reveal the emergency doctor and Willa, who still looked strange and ghastly white.

"I'd like to speak with Willa's family," the doctor announced.

"We're her family," Christine said hurriedly.

Camilla nodded and stepped back to allow the doctor to enter the hallway. She then shut the door closed between them to allow Christine, Susan, and the doctor privacy.

"What is your relation to the patient?" the doctor asked.

"She's our aunt," Susan offered, her voice high-pitched with disbelief.

"But we never knew her before yesterday," Christine admitted. "She appeared on the island, already just as confused as she is right now."

"My current diagnosis is that she's in a state of psychosis," the doctor informed them.

"Psychosis?" Christine formed the word timidly.

"She has created a world in her mind that doesn't quite exist," the doctor continued. "But psychoses come in many different sorts and are caused by many different things. You said that you didn't know her prior to this episode, which means that this very well could be a frequent event in this woman's life. That said, psychoses also can be brought on by stress or certain types of trauma."

Christine and Susan exchanged worried glances. This was above Christine's comprehension. Depression, anxiety, even dementia... she understood the many facets of these diseases and disorders, but psychosis? This was another ballgame.

"I'm going to recommend a really wonderful psychiatrist here on the Vineyard," he informed them. "I'll have Camilla make the call for you and arrange for an appointment this week. I've prescribed her lurasidone to calm her down a bit— but not enough for a full treatment plan. That will have to come through the psychiatrist herself."

Susan thanked the doctor before he marked something on Willa's clipboard and passed it back through the door to give to Camilla.

"It's a good thing you brought her in when you did," the doctor said. "I've seen similar episodes go south very quickly."

As though he'd just remarked on the weather, rather than their aunt's mental state, the doctor then turned around on his white tennis shoes and squeaked back down the hallway to yet another waiting emergency.

Susan slapped her hands across her thighs distractedly. "I guess that means we don't know a whole lot more than what we did before."

Christine stepped through the doorway to greet Willa, who gave them a sleepy smile.

"I can feel it right now," Willa said as she pointed to her forehead. "Feel the intrusive thoughts. I can feel how wrong they are."

Christine searched Nurse Camilla's eyes, hunting for some sign of what to do next. The mind was a strange thing. But all

Camilla could do was say, "I'll call you first thing when I have an appointment set up for Willa."

They drove back to Susan's place in stunned silence. Even Willa seemed to know better than to speak, as though she suspected that anything she said wouldn't actually exist in the real world. Christine tried to put herself in Willa's shoes. Without a doubt, it was a terrifying thing to be unable to trust the inner workings of your mind.

Lola arrived with baby Max as Christine stepped out of the back of Susan's Prius. Perhaps it was the lack of sleep; perhaps it was the stress. Something within her felt out of balance. She pressed a hand across her stomach and admitted to her sisters that she needed to lie down for a little bit back at the Sheridan house. Lola looked at her with a look of exasperation, which was immediately replaced with tenderness.

"Yes, of course. You must be exhausted," she commented. "We'll just be here. Come on by when you can."

Aunt Kerry and Grandpa Wes sat in the living room of the Sheridan house, as Amanda had already left for her job up at the Law Offices of Sheridan and Sheridan. Christine walked past them as Aunt Kerry asked Wes, "She must have been no more than nine when she left the island?"

"A few years older, but not by much," Wes affirmed contemplatively. "It really broke Anna up inside when her parents took Willa away."

"Christine! Did you just take Willa to the hospital?" Aunt Kerry demanded, her eyes cat-like.

"We did," Christine replied as she placed her hand timidly on the staircase railing. "She doesn't know quite what year it is."

"Welcome to the club," Wes joked. Kerry swatted him and said, "Stop that."

"I have to lie down for a while," Christine told them. "But I'm sure Susan will cook up a big breakfast over there if you're interested. You know our Susie. She'll cook something up for everyone, even at the end of the world."

Christine forced herself back to her childhood bedroom, where she again collapsed as her stomach shifted into another strange cramp. She had read endlessly about labor across countless message boards on the internet. She'd typed silly questions into the search engine, demanding things like, "Is it normal to want to murder your partner at five months?" and, "When will the swelling in my ankles and feet subside?" and, "What does childbirth feel like?" Normally, she didn't remember the answers to her questions and she knew it was all a normal part of the nesting phase, but she wanted to be completely prepared, although Christine knew that would never happen.

Now that her strange cramps had kicked up in the midst of the Willa disaster, Christine again lifted her phone to type:

"Is it real labor, or is it stress?"

A number of options popped up, including one site that said, "Although it's not totally clear what the connection between stress and labor is, it's clear that women who experience a great deal of stress often go into labor earlier."

Christine's heartbeat quickened to the speed of a rabbit's. She pressed her hand over her mouth, realizing that even her reading this had elevated her stress levels. She tossed her phone to the far end of the bed and stared at the sultry nineties face of Alanis Morrissett.

"Tell me I'm not going to have the baby early, Alanis," Christine whispered. "Tell me I still have time."

Unfortunately, Christine's stomach seized with another jolt of pain, even as Alanis's glazed expression seemed to translate the truth: neither Alanis nor Christine had a say in when this baby was coming. This baby planned to do whatever it wanted.

Chapter Six

Three and a half months before, when Lola, Max, and Christine had helped Audrey move into her small room in the putrid-green house on West Beaver Avenue, just south of Penn State's campus, Audrey had been the personification of optimism. "Become a renowned journalist. Write the truth. Make my son as proud of me as I can." This had been her sort of mantra. It was laughable, now.

On move-in day, after the bed was made and the desk placed in the center of the long wall, Lola had procured a little gift with a light shrug. "What's that, Mom? A cheesy inspirational quote?" Audrey had asked at the time, always the first to plant a joke.

To this, Lola had rolled her eyes, placed a nail directly over the wall over Audrey's desk, and hammered it in. Each whack of the hammer against the nail had dinged through Audrey's head. Lola then slipped the framed picture over the nail, stepped back, and inspected her work.

"It's just a little something to make you feel more at home

here," Lola had whispered at the time. "Just a little something to remind you how important all this is. Not just for yourself and your career, but for the world, as well."

Within the glorious mahogany frame was a quote, written in calligraphy.

"Journalism can never be silent: that is its greatest virtue and its greatest fault. It must speak, and speak immediately, while the echoes of wonder, the claims of triumph, and the signs of horror are still in the air."

The quote was attributed to Henry Anatole Grunwald, the once-managing editor of *Time Magazine*. He'd been born in Austria in 1922 before arriving in the United States in 1940, avoiding potential death back in Europe as World War II raged on. Within his life, Henry Anatole Grunwald had fought diligently in pursuit of the immediacy of truth.

And apparently, Lola thought Audrey had a similar vision for her life.

For a long while, Audrey had upheld that vision for herself. She could remember it sizzling within her as she'd stayed up late nights, nursing Max back to sleep. His large blue eyes had peered up at her as she'd swam with regret and fear about her return to Penn State. "It'll all be worth it. For the both of us," she'd whispered to him at the time.

How silly to be a twenty-year-old woman speaking nonsense to a baby boy far past midnight. Yet, it had seemed so truthful at the time.

Nearly everything had changed since summertime. That quote remained above Audrey's desk, mocking the rest of her messed-up existence.

Out in the living room of the little house that Audrey shared with three other twenty-year-old girls, a glass smashed across the floor, which caused another of her roommates to shriek outright.

"Oh my God! Is it broken?" This was the voice of Audrey's freshman-year best friend, Cassie, whom she'd met in the dorms one late Saturday morning, when they'd both been hungry for burritos.

Audrey blinked glazed eyes toward her journalism textbook and pressed her hands over her ears. The following morning was her last final of the semester, a real doozy that began at eight in the morning and stretched on till eleven. The test itself consisted of multiple-choice, short essay, and long-form essay questions. Audrey had viewed this particular final as the greatest impending doom of her already torrentially dark semester. Here it was— and she couldn't focus to save her life.

The front door screamed open. A male voice called out, "Cassie? We got the beer!"

"Put it on the back porch!" Cassie called back.

Audrey groaned and smacked her hands across her cheeks. Recently, Cassie had begun dating Matt, a member of the Sigma Nu fraternity, and he'd taken to bringing his friends around after class to "chill" with Cassie, Quinn, and Hannah, the women of the green house on West Beaver.

There was a rap on Audrey's bedroom door. She shook her head almost violently and stared at the handle. A little voice within her said, *"if that door opens, I swear, I'll scream."*

But in a moment, Nate, Matt's best bud from the frat, appeared in the crack of Audrey's doorway. He had a wad of blonde hair atop his head and a terrible neck beard— but he wasn't entirely bad-looking, especially not for a twenty-year-old boy. In recent months, he'd taken a real liking to Audrey, and

Audrey had rejected his advances, even going so far, one night, as to tell him, "Nate, dude. I have a baby." To this, he'd just replied, "That's hot."

"What can I do for you, Nate?" Audrey asked then as she folded her arms over her chest.

"Aud, come on, man. You've spent all semester cooped up in this room." Nate's smile was infectious, featuring his enormous set of bright white teeth, which his parents had almost assuredly paid for with several years of braces.

"And I have just one more final before I can escape," she told him.

Nate's smile widened to produce a deep dimple in his right cheek. Had Audrey never had Max or gone off to the Vineyard or met Noah, would she have gotten involved with this sort of college guy? Maybe. And probably, it would have been nice, in its own, innocent way.

"Audrey! Hey!" Cassie appeared beside Nate with shards of glass placed delicately on her outstretched palm.

"I see you took out another wine glass," Audrey said.

"I told you. Red solo cups are the only cups you need," Nate informed Cassie, who rolled her eyes flirtatiously before returning her gaze to Audrey.

"Are you coming out tonight? We're going to pre-game here and then hit up the bars. Nate and Matt just got us a few fake IDs, but they normally don't even check during the week."

"I have a final, Cass." Audrey ran her fingers through her hair distractedly. Had her roommates spent a single evening at home with a book open in front of them? Had they given a single thought to the importance of their education? Jealousy (mixed with a fair amount of regret) surged through Audrey.

"Right, but maybe tomorrow night?" Cassie asked.

"Don't you have tests this week?" Audrey asked.

"Naw. I just have to finish a paper, and then I'm home free."

"Our girl's a creative writing major," Matt called from within the living room, where he seemed to be in the midst of setting up the table for beer pong. "She doesn't need to use that head of hers."

"Stop!" Cassie shrieked and whipped back around to "deal" with Matt, who instead took the shards of glass off of her and placed them in the neighboring trashcan with a flippant motion.

"You know, we're going to need more people for the beer pong tournament," Nate told her firmly, as though her inclusion in that was life or death.

"I'm sure you can handle it without me," she told him. "Now, will you please shut my door?"

Nate finally did as he was told. Audrey leaped up, grabbed a towel, and spread it out beneath the crack in the door in an attempt to eliminate the noise. As it was finals week, the library was rammed with other studying individuals and similarly distracting; any coffee shop would probably be just as bad, with the addition of bad coffee and stale snacks. Audrey felt herself in a sort of trap of her own making. Outside the door, Matt roared that Cassie had to "drink the whole cup!" which led their other roommate, Quinn, to wail with laughter. Audrey's head spun with distraction.

Audrey grabbed her cell and flipped through her contacts, on the hunt for some sort of comfort in the whirlwind that was unfolding in front of her. Her fingers paused for a moment over Noah's name as her heart drummed with sorrow. Since their interaction at Thanksgiving, Noah had given her the distance she'd craved. He hadn't called, hadn't texted. As far as she knew, he hadn't thought of her at all.

How childish she now felt, praying to the moon and the stars that he would write her again.

On cue, her phone buzzed with a text from her mother.

Lola: Hi, honey! I just wanted to let you know. We've taken Christine up to the hospital. We think she might have the baby tonight.

Audrey's eyes widened with panic. This was too soon, wasn't it? Perhaps three weeks too soon. Flashing images of the NICU raced through her mind.

Homesickness and fear brought her finger to the CALL button. She pressed her phone against her ear as the phone rang out toward that island in the middle of the inky-black ocean. After six rings, there was still nothing. A moment later, Lola wrote back.

Lola: Sorry, honey. I'm just with Christine and her doctor. I'll call you back as soon as I can.

Audrey's heart hammered in her chest with apprehension. She stood and stomped out the door of her bedroom, where she discovered Cassie, Quinn, Nate, and Matt in the midst of a chaotic beer pong session. Cassie's blue eyes were hazy, and the air reeked of cheap beer. Their other roommate, Hannah, texted furiously, her body stretched out along the red couch.

They were the perfect portrait of a college TV sitcom ensemble.

Audrey, the single mother with a broken heart, just didn't fit the picture before her.

"What's up, Aud?" Cassie smiled sweetly, waving the bruised-looking ping pong ball through the air.

"You look like you saw a ghost," Nate countered.

Audrey longed to tell him how silly he sounded but instead directed her body down the hallway and into the bathroom, where the shower was consistently lined with at least three months of gunk and grime and girls' body hair. Audrey closed the toilet and sat at the edge, her toes against the ground as she teetered to and fro. Her brain had zero comprehension of what journalism even meant any longer. Christine was on the verge of the biggest chapter in her life thus far and Audrey was trapped in this dank, putrid-green house on West Beaver Avenue. She felt misplaced.

After a small, intimate cry, Audrey escaped the bathroom to find that now, only Nate and Hannah played beer pong, while Quinn, Matt, and Cassie sat cross-legged on the floor in front of a bottle of vodka. Matt pressed his blue tooth speaker on, and immediately, Red Hot Chili Peppers roared through their small space.

"I love this one," he told Cassie, who looked at him as though he'd written the song himself.

"Could you guys keep it down out here?" Audrey tried.

Quinn made a strange noise in her throat, lifted her finger, and dropped the volume down three notches, which was hardly anything at all in the grand scheme of things. Perhaps this was all Audrey would get.

When she retreated back into her room, however, someone pumped up the volume once again. "Californication" became the rasping cry of this last horrible night before the final that very well could make or break Audrey's career. It was almost laughable, all the absurdness that swirled around her.

As she waited for her mother's call, Audrey thought long and hard about dialing Noah just to say hello. It had been rude of her to cut things off entirely. He had been something of an anchor for her throughout her months in Pennsylvania— texting her funny memes throughout the day, giving her assurance that she'd done the right thing in coming back, and even sending flowers and take-out food at random. Cassie had teased that Noah was the "perfect boyfriend," as he cared for her in every feasible way without demanding too much of her time or her energy. How had Audrey screwed it up so badly?

Finally, Lola called back.

"Mom?" Audrey's voice was strained with worry.

"Hi, honey."

In the background, Max cooed and screeched. Audrey's heart surged with love and confusion. Her body quaked. That was her baby, in another woman's arms. That was her baby to care for.

"We're still waiting a bit longer here at the hospital, but the doctor's pretty sure it's Braxton Hicks. They're monitoring the contractions now to see," Lola continued.

"So, no baby yet?" Audrey breathed.

"No, but Christine might have to be put on bedrest. She's not exactly thrilled about that."

"I can imagine," Audrey returned as her eyes welled with tears.

Max's screeches transformed into cries, and Audrey's heart jumped into her throat at the sounds of her child.

"Can you put the phone up to him so I can talk to him?" Audrey asked.

"What was that, honey? I can't hear you. Max is crying."

Audrey's nostrils flared with sorrow. "I know. I just... maybe I could talk to him? Calm him down?" Wasn't this precisely the sort of thing Audrey was meant to do?

"I don't think he'll be able to hear you, Aud. I have to let you go. I think he needs a change. I'll text you when we know more about Christine, okay? I love you."

With a dramatic clip, Lola ended the call and left Audrey standing there in her own silence, yet again, in the off-shoot of the beer-reeking living room. Audrey kicked her desk hard, trying to let some of her frustrations out. This shook the wall and caused the frame above the desk to yank leftward, becoming crooked. Audrey didn't have the strength to fix it.

She returned her eyes to her textbook, her pen poised. But already, it was seven-thirty in the evening and the roar from the living room seemed never-ending. How would she barrel through this horrendous night? How would she possibly work through the final in the morning?

You just will, a voice within her told her. You just will.

And as Nate dunked yet another ping pong in a big vat of foamy beer outside, Audrey forced her pen to paper and began to take much-needed notes. She knew deep down that it would be a long night.

Chapter Seven

Christine's eyes opened at the first sign of the glorious December morning. Sunlight streamed through the small crack in the drapes as Zach rustled around in the soft grey shadows. There was something about watching someone you love's early-morning routine— something intimate about knowing in which order they showered, made coffee, brushed their teeth, and put on cologne, that Christine hadn't reckoned for when she'd decided to link her life forever with Zach Walters. Always, love was about the little things. She wasn't sure why this always seemed such a surprise to her. Perhaps the surprise, in and of itself, was a gift.

When Zach turned back to face her, he buttoned the tip-top of his shirt and gave her a fatigued yet still handsome smile. Christine spread her palm across her ballooning belly and breathed, "Good morning, baby."

"That was quite a night," Zach said as he stepped toward the bed and pressed a kiss upon her forehead. "I thought for sure we'd be parents by this morning."

"Me too." Exhaustion folded over her at the memory of the previous afternoon and evening as Lola and Susan had rushed her off to the hospital. She'd been a red-faced, anxious wreck, totally panicked and squeezing Lola's fingers to a mashed pulp. Up at the hospital, she had learned that the contractions were simply Braxton Hicks, which were a practice round of pre-labor for her body and very normal, the doctor had explained. Eventually, she'd been sent home with a, *"We'll see you soon!"* This had sounded far more sinister than they'd meant it to.

In truth, this "practice round" had escalated Christine's worries in nearly every dimension. Childbirth hadn't been a thing she'd ever envisioned herself to do. Now, it rushed toward her, promising searing pain, with potential complications, and an entirely new baby to care for— all in one fell swoop.

"We have a little bit of time, so I don't want you to worry," Zach said softly. "But I spoke with Susan, and we've decided that you should spend the next few days over at her place while I finish up everything at the Bistro. It's just easier that way and she can keep an eye on you if anything happens."

Christine groaned inwardly and dropped her head back against the pillow.

"The doctor said bedrest. Somebody has to be around to make that bedrest easier on you. You know, to fetch you Christmas cookies and fluff your pillows and..."

"I'm not a princess, Zach. I'm just pregnant." Christine's joke fell flat.

"I just want to make sure you're well-taken-care-of," Zach told her, his nostrils flared. "And unfortunately, I haven't yet trained the cat to be able to do that."

"That's on you. You took all those cat training classes for a reason." Christine grumbled the joke as Zach headed back toward the hallway. The familiar whistle of the kettle bellowed through the house.

Christine's phone buzzed with a message from Lola.

LOLA: Taking Willa to her first emergency psychiatric appointment this morning.

LOLA: We'll meet you back at Susan's after?

CHRISTINE: Sounds like I'll be a permanent fixture on the couch.

LOLA: Don't worry, Mama. We'll take good care of you.

A half-hour later, Zach helped Christine walk at a snail's pace all the way to the minivan, where she slipped into the backseat and lay back with her knees bent toward the car ceiling. Zach buzzed through radio stations until he settled on a Christmas-only station, which currently played "Silent Night."

As they drove across Oak Bluffs, Christine and Zach remained quiet, allowing the music to wash over them. Christine often wondered about Zach's internal monologue during this strange, intimate, and terrifying time. After all, he'd already done the fatherhood thing, a time that had resulted in tragedy. His daughter had died in a horrible accident. Assuredly, he was even more frightened than Christine was, if only because he'd already felt the brevity of loss.

To his credit, Zach had worked diligently to ensure that he was mentally and emotionally prepared for this next round of fatherhood. He spoke of his previous child infrequently— hints here and there that he'd spent some time watching silly childhood movies or had lost a whole year of his life due to "sleepless nights." It was a strange thing to know that your life partner had lived entire chapters prior to your union with them. Christine, too, had had her other chapters.

It was their choice to write this next one together.

When Christine and Zach reached the entry for the long driveway that snaked through the trees and led toward Susan's cabin-like home, Zach announced that Lola had come from the opposite direction. Christine lifted a hand through the space between the front seats to wave. Lola beeped the horn gently.

Zach parked the van behind Lola and then pulled open the back door to assist Christine onto the gravel driveway.

"You remember Christine, don't you, Willa?" This was Lola, whose voice seemed overly bright, as though she thought she could keep everything together with enough positivity.

"Oh, yes. Of course. Anna's second daughter?" Willa sounded as though she had just awoken from a dream.

Christine stood on shaky legs with Zach's hand stretched out across her back. She lent Willa a warm smile as Lola hustled back to help Zach guide Christine to the back door.

"Come on, you two," Christine teased. "It's not like I've forgotten how to walk."

Willa headed up the little path that led to the back door. Kellan opened it just before she knocked, which resulted in Willa leaping back fearfully. Kellan blinked at her, confused, his coat on and his backpack strapped across his shoulders.

"Hi, Willa," he said coaxingly. "I didn't mean to frighten you."

Willa strung her fingers through her hair, then stepped around the teenager and headed into the house like a frightened animal.

"Don't mind her," Lola told Kellan under her breath. "She's

just a bit all over the place right now. The doctor says it's a psychotic episode. Her brain has made up a story about her reality and she's currently a slave to it until the meds kick in."

Kellan's eyes widened as Christine, Lola, and Zach ambled past him. This was a whole lot more than a teenager wanted to deal with during the hour before first period.

Susan rushed out of the back door right then, waving a bright white piece of paper. "Kellan! You forgot your permission slip!"

Kellan hustled back, grabbed the paper, thanked his step-mother, and then rushed back out onto the main road. Seconds later, they heard the monstrous gasp of the school bus as it paused on the main road to pick him up.

"Look at you, Stepmom," Christine teased as her smile blossomed.

Susan waved a hand to and fro. Christine knew that Susan had been rather fearful about Kellan's decision to live with Scott and Susan rather than his mother in Boston. Kellan had seemed the antithesis of everything Susan had wanted to build in her "fresh start on the Vineyard." In recent months, however, Kellan had become a marvelous pupil, a kind step-grandson for Wes, and a hilarious little cousin to Amanda and Audrey. He fit in ways Christine hadn't fit until her early forties.

Susan and Amanda had created a cozy little ecosystem for Christine's "bedrest" in the living room. The couch was stuffed with fluffed pillows and fuzzy blankets; a little basket alongside the couch was filled with some of Christine's favorite healthy (and not-so-healthy) snacks; a glass of carbonated water with lemon awaited her. Zach eased Christine into place on the couch and then splayed a bright yellow blanket across her legs and stomach.

"Snug as a bug in a rug," he said playfully.

Willa sat in the chair, kitty-corner to Christine. She seemed oddly listless as she chewed at the edge of a crunchy pretzel, her eyes glazed over. The previous afternoon, when Christine had been up at the hospital with Lola and Susan, Amanda and Wes had babysat Willa. According to Amanda, the three of them had sat in front of the television and watched DVD after DVD until Willa had admitted that she needed to sleep. Despite their history, Wes and Willa hadn't wanted to say much to one another. Lola had suggested this was because Willa's psychosis had confused her so much that she couldn't connect the current Wes Sheridan with the previous version of him. As Wes was still exhausted, he hadn't pushed it.

After Zach drove back to the Bistro, Wes, Amanda, and Baby Max arrived at Susan's place with a large box of Frosted Delight donuts. Frosted Delights was a sinfully delicious bakery over in Edgartown, operated by Jennifer Conrad and her mother, Ariane. As Christine was a trained pastry chef, her palate was often a picky one when it came to baked goods. In her mind, miraculously, the Frosted Delights passed the test.

"There she is. My darling daughter," Wes greeted Christine tenderly as his eyes welled with tears. "I thought for darn sure I'd have myself another grand baby last night."

"Me too," Christine returned. "Guess you'll have to put up with just me a little bit longer."

Amanda bounced Max playfully in her arms as Susan placed a maple-cream donut on a plate for Christine.

"Willa? Would you like a donut?" Christine asked gently.

"Willa, you must know this place," Wes said. "Frosted Delights Bakery over in Edgartown."

"That's right. It's a staple of the community." Susan lifted a simple glazed donut to her lips. "It's been around for decades."

"Frosted Delights?" Willa batted her eyelashes. Her cheeks glowed bright pink, as though she was some kind of doll. "Yes. I think Anna used to bring me there."

"I'm sure she did," Wes affirmed. "Anna was a real sucker for donuts or anything sweet, for that matter. That woman had such a sweet tooth."

Christine's heart dropped into her stomach. This talk about Anna Sheridan felt like looking too long at the sun. Christine's heart ached for a woman she'd never see again; she reckoned with the immensity of a loss that had occurred so long ago that she could hardly remember the sound of her voice.

"I need to take a nap," Willa said suddenly. She rose from the chair with robotic motions, then turned herself back toward the guest room.

"We'll save you a donut, Willa," Lola told her. "Get some rest."

The entire Sheridan clan kept their mouths closed tightly until the upstairs guest room door clipped shut. Wes stepped toward the cozy chair Willa had vacated and collapsed in it. His donut remained hardly touched on the china plate on his lap.

"What do you remember about Willa from those days?" Christine asked her father then.

Wes's eyes closed to reveal the delicacy of his eyelids, which seemed as thin as a butterfly's wing.

"She was such a sweet little thing when I first met her," Wes breathed. "I think it was outside of the high school. She was maybe eight or nine and wanted to show off her cartwheels. At the time, I was a bit annoyed. Why did I have to sit around with my girlfriend and watch this little young thing whip around the grass? But Anna was overjoyed with everything she did. She would clap her hands wildly as though Willa was actually a gymnast in the Olympics or something. It was one of the first moments that I realized Anna would be a brilliant mother one day."

Wes shook his head again as he lifted his donut. "It's hard for me to align this current version of Willa with that little girl. How is it possible that they're one and the same?"

"Do you have any idea of why she might have sought us out right now?" Lola asked. "Or any idea of where her psychosis might have come from?"

"Did her parents have any history of mental illness?" Susan asked.

Wes considered this for a moment as he blew the air out of his mouth, making his cheeks puff out. "Your mother wasn't a big fan of her parents. She kept away from them as much as she could, especially after we officially moved in together. That all happened in a great rush. There was a fight with her mother. Things were said that they couldn't come back from."

Christine, Lola, and Susan exchanged glances. History and time seemed generational. In previous eras, they had thought that they would never speak to Wes Sheridan again. They'd rebounded from that pain and sorrow and separation, somehow. Thank goodness.

"Things were different back then," Wes continued. "Mental illness wasn't as talked about. Perhaps Anna's mother was more than just a drunk. Back then, people just called her crazy. In any case, Anna's mother threatened her time and again not to come around Willa's school to check up on her. She told her to stay away. And then, she tried to use Willa as a kind of bait to get to see

68

you, Susan, after you were born. Naturally, this enraged your mother. She was terribly protective, as all mothers are."

The Sheridan family again held the silence as Wes's story fell over them like a blanket of snow. It seemed incredible that these family secrets had remained lodged in the past for forty-five years.

"To answer your question, Lola, I haven't a clue why she's here," Wes admitted. "Anna and I never heard from her after she left the island. Anna cried about it frequently in those early years but soon tucked that pain back behind other pains. That's what you must do to survive, after all. Choose your damage. And we were so busy with you three girls and the Sunrise Cove and the Bistro and..." He shook his head as his eyes darkened.

"The doctor said that it might take her some time to understand where this psychosis came from..." Lola said finally.

"She's really like a ghost," Wes breathed. "When I first heard her voice on the phone at the Sunrise Cove, looking for me, I thought maybe I was having some kind of episode. It really took me out of myself. And now that she's here, confused about what year it is— like me, sometimes, it's like a version of time travel. Like in many ways, if we close our eyes and shift our perception just a little bit, the year is still 1980, and everyone we love and hold dear is still alive."

Chapter Eight

Audrey awoke that morning at 7:55 a.m., precisely five minutes before the start of her very important, future-altering final exam, which she had spent the previous night cramming for. She burst from her bed, a sweaty, fearful mess, and scrambled for her sweatshirt, a pair of jeans, two mismatched socks, and her tennis shoes. By 7:58 a.m., she pounded through the living room, where the air was milkshake-thick with the rancid smell of beer and cigarettes. A stranger was stretched out on the couch, his mouth open and snoring. Another was on the floor.

The building where the final exam was held was a fifteen-minute walk from Audrey's putrid-green house. Audrey stretched her legs out before her, her heart squeezing with panic as she hustled through the intersections and whipped onto the beautiful campus, a place she had fallen head-over-heels with two years before, as a young eighteen-year-old with optimism as her only currency.

Against all laws of physics, Audrey arrived at the door of the final exam by 8:10 a.m., only ten minutes late. She gasped for breath, gripped her knees, and blinked at the floor as dark and light spots swirled through her vision. As she steadied herself, her brain ran through a list of facts she'd deemed necessary for the exam ahead.

"Hunter S. Thompson. Pavel Sheremet. Veronica Guerin..." She paced out the names of famous journalists as her mind ascribed their contributions to the field. "Neil Budde. Anna Politkovskaya..."

There was only one way to become the journalist she'd always dreamed of being— and that only way existed on the other side of this door.

Audrey tugged herself upright, wrapped a hand around the handle of the door, and tried to open it. Her stomach tightened when she pushed and it didn't budge. After a moment's pause, she rapped her knuckles against the door, realizing that she'd already lost twelve minutes of the three-hour test. Every moment counted.

Loud footsteps rushed toward her. Her professor appeared in the crack of the door and blinked down at her with disdain etched across her face.

"Audrey... There you are."

Audrey gave her professor a sheepish smile. The professor remained in the crack of the doorway for a split second before slipping out of the room, where she remained between Audrey and the rest of the class.

"Audrey, I told you and the other students. It's essential that you arrive on time."

"I know, but I accidentally slept through my alarm."

The professor shrugged her pointed shoulders. "I don't see how that's my problem."

Audrey froze, panicked as a deer in the middle of the road with an eighteen-wheeler speeding directly toward her.

"You have to let me take the test," Audrey pleaded. "I haven't missed a single class since the start of the semester. I've—I've turned in all my papers, and I've been involved in class discussions, and I've…"

"You mean you've done the bare minimum?" The professor arched her eyebrow cruelly.

"I studied for this exam all night while my roommates partied up a storm," Audrey whispered.

"I'm certain that you did," the professor told her. "And I'm also certain that I can't let you into this room to take the test. If you ever become a journalist, you'll understand. You can't be late for a press conference. You can't be late for an interview. You must find your scoop and be eternally committed to it. That doesn't mean sleeping through your alarm. It sometimes means staying up all night, just to track down your story."

Audrey was gobsmacked. Her lips parted with shock, but no words spilled out.

"Now, if you'll excuse me, I have to head back in to watch the rest of the students finish out their final exam," the professor continued, adding insult to injury. "Your grade will be listed by the end of the week."

"But without the final exam, I won't come out of this with anything better than a C," Audrey murmured, her voice hardly a whisper.

"A C is a passing grade," the professor told her. "It's better than nothing." She then turned on her heel and stepped back into the sinisterly quiet classroom, where students Audrey had studied and worked alongside for months curled their necks forward and wrote essay after essay.

Audrey hadn't felt this low in a long, long time. With the door closed tightly between herself and her potential future, she crumpled into a ball and fell against the wall. A single wail escaped her lips, but she soon clapped a hand over her mouth. The last thing she needed was for the professor to jump out of the classroom and demand that she move on so as not to distract the other students.

When Audrey drummed up the strength to leave the university building, she walked into a winter wonderland of a campus. Fluffy white snowflakes fell from the heavens and lined the sidewalks and the tops of the trees. Audrey couldn't engage with its beauty. Her eyesight was blurred from her tears.

When Audrey entered her house once more, she found Cassie and Quinn in the midst of cooking breakfast for all the drinking stragglers from the previous night. Their eyes were shadowed, and even their skin seemed to reek of alcohol. Still, their laughter rang out joyously as they clanked around the kitchen.

"Is that Audrey?" Cassie cried, a spatula lifted.

"How did your test go?" Quinn asked.

Audrey might have told Quinn that her last night's lipstick had streaked across her cheek had she had more physical strength.

"It went okay," Audrey lied.

"You were a studying machine last night," Cassie said. "Nate was heartbroken, as usual."

"But I keep telling him that you're dating that hottie from the island," Quinn said.

"That's just because you've got a big crush on Nate." Cassie stated playfully, letting the cat out of the bag.

"Shut up. I do not," Quinn retorted as her cheeks tinged red.

"We'll make you a plate," Cassie informed Audrey.

"No. Don't worry. I just need to sleep." Audrey turned on her heel and headed straight for her bedroom. Once inside, she closed the door and rushed toward the framed quote about journalism and ripped it off the wall. She then hid it behind her desk, her heart beating wildly.

Audrey then collapsed, fully clothed, on her bed and stared at the ceiling. The muffled voices from the living room and the kitchen seemed a part of another world, one that she no longer had access to. She was just a washed-up student, a washed-up mother, and in her eyes, a general failure. Other students, like Cassie and Quinn, could make a million little mistakes. The stakes weren't as high for them. They didn't have a son waiting for them at home.

Mid-afternoon, Audrey checked her phone to find several messages from her mother and an email from her journalism school counselor.

LOLA: Tomorrow! Tomorrow! It's only a day away.

LOLA: I think we'll be able to get there by two or three in the afternoon. I think we'll stay the night halfway to keep things light and easy for us.

Audrey's eyes closed against the turmoil of this. Soon, she would have to explain to her mother the depths of her failure.

And what would she do, now that her journalism career was over before it had even begun? Perhaps Amanda and Susan would hire her to be a secretary at the Law Offices of Sheridan and Sheridan? Perhaps Kelli would let her pick up hours at the boutique she owned? Perhaps she could make furniture with Andy and that old war veteran over in Edgartown or help Claire with flower arrangements or train with Christine to become a pastry chef?

They were all potential goals she could strive for— yet none of them seemed to ignite any excitement within her.

The email from her school counselor was even worse.

Hi Audrey,

I wanted to check in again about next semester. We have yet to meet to decide your class schedule. It would be good to have that squared away before you leave for Christmas break, especially as many classes you need for your journalism degree are filling up fast.

I hope you're having a wonderful end of the semester. It's all stressful (I know it well!), but it will be worth it.

Ms. Evans

Audrey groaned and tossed her phone toward the end of her bed. In the living room, someone, maybe Nate again, suggested that they get started early on beer pong. Audrey curved herself into another ball and willed herself into another reality. If only she'd woken up ten minutes earlier. If only she'd heard her alarm.

The following afternoon, Audrey stood out on the front porch of the putrid green house with two suitcases on either side of her and absolutely no plans to return to Pennsylvania. Her mother's car appeared through the swirling snowfall, a sign of comfort, of home. Audrey rushed down the driveway and pulled open the back door to find her darling baby, a baby who'd changed in a million different, beautiful, and heartbreaking ways since she'd last seen him on Thanksgiving. His eyelids were curled over his eyes as he slept peacefully; his little, tender hand stretched over his stomach as though he held onto himself for comfort.

"He slept almost the entire way," Lola announced as she appeared beside Audrey with a bouquet of flowers.

Audrey blinked up into her mother's gorgeous face. Her knees nearly collapsed beneath her. She fell into Lola's arms and shook as Lola whispered, "Honey, it's going to be all right," her voice soothing but heavy with confusion.

"We're here to take you home," Lola breathed as she swept a hand over Audrey's hair. "Max and I have missed you so much."

Finally, Audrey piled her suitcases into the back of her mother's car and then collapsed in the front seat. She felt none of her normal, snarky personality; she felt like the color grey. As her mother drove down West Beaver Avenue, Audrey didn't bother to glance back toward the putrid-green house.

As they drove, Lola flicked through the Christmas stations before ultimately deciding on Mariah Carey's "All I Want for Christmas is You."

"Remember when you used to belt this out in our little apartment in Boston?" Lola tried. "You wanted to try out for American Idol so bad. I'm glad you found other dreams."

Audrey could half-remember it: her up on her mother's bed, using her mother's hairbrush as a microphone as Lola pretended to be an entire audience down below.

"That life was really something," Audrey breathed.

"Just the two of us for so long," Lola replied with a smile. "It's hard to believe it. And now that we're on the island, new family members keep coming out of the woodwork."

Lola then went on to explain a bit about Audrey's Great Aunt Willa and her current state of psychosis.

"It's not bad enough that she needs to be in a hospital, thankfully," Lola said. "I can't imagine dropping someone off at a place like that, especially my mother's sister."

Audrey could feel the emotion behind her mother's words. Lola, Susan, and Christine ached for Anna Sheridan in ways that Audrey couldn't fully comprehend. Lola had been her constant lifeline, her everything. Even now, her presence as they sped back east calmed Audrey's racing heart.

"I guess we're all hoping that once she gets out of this psychotic state, she'll be able to tell us something about our mother that we never knew," Lola said finally. "We're so hungry for memories of Anna Sheridan. And it's like a little piece of her came to the Vineyard for Christmas. It's just not quite that simple. I suppose nothing ever is."

Chapter Nine

The Christmas tree at the far corner of the living room at the Sheridan house was stuffed to the gills with Christmas bulbs, homemade decorations, tinsel, beautiful star ornaments, and several hanging photographs in tiny glass frames, many of which featured Anna Sheridan and Wes Sheridan during the early stages of parenting— holding baby Susan, building a snowman with toddler Christine, or helping four-year-old Lola ride a bike.

Audrey held Max up to one particular photograph of Anna and Wes on their wedding day and whispered, "Look, Max. That's your great-granddad and great-grandmother, Wesley and Anna. Aren't they beautiful?"

Max buzzed his lips in response yet seemed to become excited by her words. He then smashed a fist against her chest playfully and burst into laughter. Susan passed by, en-route to her never-ending list of tasks in the kitchen, and greeted Max with a sing-song voice.

"There he is! It's Max's first Christmas!"

Max's eyes bugged out in greeting, and he squealed loudly and then attempted to dig his way out of Audrey's arms if only to reach out for Susan's. Audrey's heart darkened. Since their arrival to the Vineyard earlier that afternoon, she'd sensed Max's allegiance to other members of the family: the women who bathed him, fed him, played with him, and dressed him daily. Women who weren't his mother.

"Sorry, Max, honey, but I have a whole lot of hungry people to feed," Susan said playfully. "Have your people call my people, and maybe we can arrange a meeting later."

Audrey tried to laugh, but it sounded high-pitched and strange. Lola leaped out of the kitchen, where a number of pots and skillets sizzled with the approaching "Audrey's Back!" dinner of roast duck and grilled peach salad, plus broccoli and mashed potatoes and freshly-baked rolls.

"I need you in here, Susie! I'm in over my head," Lola called out.

Christine stretched out on the couch before Audrey, all wrapped up in blankets and propped up with pillows. She chewed at the corner of a Christmas cookie nervously, her eyes toward the snow-filled sky out the window. Audrey stepped toward Christine, dropped to the ground, folded her legs beneath her, and then allowed Max to roam the space between the couch and the Christmas tree. He padded around like a little explorer, captivated with every nook and cranny.

The house bustled with activity over the next several minutes, enough that Audrey felt continually quiet and listless in comparison. Kellan and Grandpa Wes appeared after a jaunt through the woods; both were red-cheeked and joyful with laughter. Scott entered the kitchen to assist Susan with the duck. Even Tommy, that burly sailor Audrey's mother had fallen head-over-heels with, appeared soon afterward, a Christmas cookie in hand and his smile nervous, which was a funny contrast to the fact that he ordinarily sailed across the great wide ocean alone. Aunt Kerry appeared shortly after with a huge pot of her famous clam chowder, and Amanda and Sam rushed in, unlinking their fingers after a split-second, as though they still wanted to pretend that they weren't romantically involved. Willa, Anna Sheridan's younger sister, sat in the corner, similarly fearful and quiet— Audrey's emotional twin, at the moment.

It felt very much that the island had gone on without Audrey while she'd proceeded to fall all over herself in Pennsylvania. Even Max sensed his mother was a loser.

Zach entered soon after and kissed Christine on the cheek, his brow furrowed with worry. "You feeling okay, honey?"

Christine nodded sleepily. She hadn't said many words to Audrey since her arrival, seemingly lost in her own anxious thoughts. Audrey had always appreciated this about Christine: she found it very difficult to pretend things were okay when they weren't.

Susan announced that it was time for dinner. This forced Scott, Zach, and Tommy into action, whipping around the living room and dining area to align extra tables and chairs. Amanda and Sam set the table flirtatiously, with Sam touching Amanda's shoulder to ask, "I can't remember. Knives on the right, or?" To this, Amanda teased, "Were you raised in a barn, Sam?" as her eyes glowed with adoration.

Audrey placed Max in his high-chair directly beside her chair at the table while the others sat, passing around wine bottles for extra pours and sipping water and commenting on just how "delicious" everything looked. Lola chimed her fork against her wine glass and remained standing as joyful laughter from the Sheridan family finally quieted. Audrey felt all the color drain from her cheeks.

"I just want to take a moment to say a few words," Lola announced as she looked at everyone around the table. "As many of you know, my daughter, Audrey, is the greatest love of my life. This year, I witnessed her take several steps forward. She gave birth to darling Max, whom we all love so much, and then went back to school to pursue her journalism degree, just like her mom. Audrey, we're so proud of you for going after what you want in this life, no matter what curveballs are thrown at you. Welcome back to the Vineyard for Christmas. We love you."

"We love you!" Susan and Amanda chimed in, their glasses lifted.

"So much," Grandpa Wes added.

Audrey nodded as her eyes filled with tears. She dropped her chin to her chest as emotions threatened to overwhelm her.

"It's just so nice to be home," she finally murmured, her heart-shattering.

The conversation soon swirled on without her. Baby Max smashed his plastic spoon against his highchair with the strength of a young percussionist. Audrey tried to feed him little bits of smashed yams and peas, but he eventually wore most of the oranges and greens across his bib. Audrey's own food remained mostly untouched.

"Maybe I should put him down for a nap," Audrey said distractedly, mostly to herself. She lifted him out of his highchair and then headed into the bedroom upstairs, a room her mother had used as a teenager. There, Susan had set up a crib for Max and splayed several fresh towels across the bed.

Once in his crib, however, Max decided it was time to have a full-scale breakdown. His little mouth stretched out, pink and violent, and his eyes squeezed out tear after tear. Audrey lifted him again, trying to calm him, yet feeling more and more self-conscious as his wails grew louder.

Maybe she'd lost her ability to care for him.

Maybe she just didn't have the skills to be a mother any longer.

Amanda suddenly appeared in the doorway of the bedroom, her smile friendly and warm.

"Need anything?" she asked tenderly.

Audrey wanted to scream at her cousin to leave her alone. Max was her baby; this was her job. But exhaustion overwhelmed her. Amanda hustled over and lifted Max from Audrey's arms. She held him loosely against her chest, with all the ease of an ordinary young mother, and then patted her hand against his back. Immediately, Max let out a satisfying belch, then sighed evenly. Amanda's eyes lightened up.

"I wondered if that was it," she said softly as she returned him to his crib.

"Oh gosh. I'm so..." Audrey couldn't come up with the appropriate word. *Grateful? Relieved? Embarrassed?* She held the silence for a moment as the words floated through her mind.

"Don't worry about it. We all need a little help from time to time," Amanda told her. She then lowered her eyebrows and said, "Are you doing okay, Aud?"

Throughout the winter, spring, and summer, Audrey and Amanda had become thick as thieves. Audrey no longer felt the intensity of that friendship. She felt like an outsider.

"I'm right as rain, Mandy," Audrey lied.

"I'm sure you're exhausted after all the studying you've been doing," Amanda said. "I can remember those long nights and early mornings well. And it's especially hard when it feels like everyone around you is partying and having fun while you're actually committed to learning."

Audrey swallowed the lump in her throat. "Just glad to be back with all of you for a little while."

Amanda's smile brightened. She then grabbed the baby monitor from the bedside table and said, "Come on. Let's get back down there. Tis the season for seconds, thirds, and heaps of Christmas cookies. I couldn't enjoy it that much last year since Chris had me convinced I was going to be a blushing bride the next month. My, how things change!"

"Where is Chris these days?" Audrey asked.

Amanda laughed. "He just wrote me from Beijing of all places. He said he wants to be a DJ. I mean, this was the Chris who talked to me for hours about our 401Ks."

"He's running after his dreams," Audrey joked.

"It's just funny that you can feel like you know people so well and they never reveal to you that actually, they want to run away and become a DJ in China." Amanda said. "How crazy is that?"

Back downstairs, Audrey forced herself through the rest of her meal, even finding ways to laugh and joke with Grandpa Wes, like old times. Although her mother had told her about the story of finding him out on the docks, confused and searching for Willa, he now seemed like a whip-smart intellectual, quick with a joke or a tease, for Audrey especially. It was a remarkable thing that Audrey and her grandfather had been allowed so much time alone throughout her pregnancy. She'd essentially been locked inside that very house, ballooning and eating Christine's croissants. It all seemed, now like somebody else's life.

After dinner, Audrey disappeared into the kitchen to take a breather. There, she spread her hands out atop the counter and exhaled all the oxygen from her lungs. Susan was in the midst of a story about her new law partner, Bruce, who'd recently taken on a case for a fashionable celebrity who lived part-time on the island. "But Bruce is all macho and no-nonsense. So when this girl told him how many social media followers she had, he gave her a blank look and just said, 'What does that have to do with anything?' You should have seen this poor girl's face. Social media is her bread and butter!"

The table erupted with laughter. Amanda soon picked up where her mother left off, describing what had happened with the celebrity in the foyer immediately after her meeting with Bruce and Susan. Her heart pumping with anxiety, Audrey filled herself a glass of wine, nearly to the brim, closed her eyes, and tossed her head back. She'd avoided alcohol throughout the majority of the semester, as her friends had partied deep into the night. What had it gotten her? Nothing.

When Audrey stepped back out into the kitchen, clutching her second glass of wine, she found Christine alone on the couch yet again, while the rest of the family bobbed around in little pods, deep in conversation. Even Zach was in the midst of what sounded like a sports-obsessed conversation with Kellan and Scott.

"Mind if I sit with you for a sec?" Audrey asked Christine softly.

Christine blinked up at her, her face lined with exhaustion. "The great Audrey Sheridan would actually sit with her huge pregnant, tired old aunt?"

Audrey rolled her eyes and snuggled into the little space beyond Christine's feet. Her shoulders sagged low as she eyed Amanda, who still held onto Max's baby monitor. Shouldn't that have been hers to carry?

"How are you doing, Audrey?" Christine asked it as though she'd already sensed the answer behind Audrey's stoic face.

"Just fine," Audrey lied. "And you?"

Christine's smile was sneaky. "Just fine," she echoed.

Audrey dropped her head back on the top of the couch so that her locks flowed over the back. She finally forced herself to make eye contact with Christine. Her eyes sizzled with urgency.

"You sound fine," Audrey pointed out sarcastically.

"So do you," Christine returned.

"This conversation doesn't seem to be going anywhere," Audrey said.

"You got somewhere else to be?"

Audrey's nostrils flared. She knew better than to hide from her Aunt Christine, a woman who had fallen into depths of despair, herself. It was obvious that she could spot them within someone else.

"Oh, Aud. You had a hard few months, didn't you?"

Audrey blinked back tears but made no motion of her head. Admittance of what had happened would make it the truth. Christine allowed the silence to stretch between them for another minute more as the other Sheridans around the living room and dining room belted out laughter and silly jokes.

"It feels like a ticking time bomb," Christine breathed finally.

Audrey shifted her head to catch Christine's eye again. "What do you mean?"

"This baby. The past few months, I've had nightmares almost

constantly about how inadequate I am as a mother. I worry about everything. I worry that my baby will have all the same troubles I did, mentally and emotionally and socially. I worry that my baby won't be healthy. I worry that Zach will bail again. Gosh, if there's a possible worry to have, I've had it."

Audrey stretched a hand over Christine's knee and squeezed gently. For once, it was good to focus on someone else's pain rather than her own.

"You're going to be such a good mother, Christine. You've wanted this for years. It's such a beautiful thing."

Christine arched her brow and bowed her head. "I hope you're right. But you know that no matter how many times you tell me that, I'll still have the sneaking suspicion that you're wrong."

Audrey sighed and turned her eyes toward the ground.

"Whatever it is, Audrey, you'll get through it," Christine said then, her voice low.

But Audrey just shook her head, her mind clouded. "You know how many times you tell me that, I'll still have the sneaking suspicions that you're wrong," she echoed.

"Touché," Christine returned, giving her a sneaky smile.

Chapter Ten

The living room at the Sheridan house glowed with soft orange light. The evening's festivities now dwindled; darkness seemed ever-present out the large bay window, which outlined an inky-black ocean and a dark, thick expanse of trees, there between Susan and Scott's property and the main house. Susan, Scott, and Kellan had just snuck through those very trees, armed with their fair share of leftovers, while now, Zach helped Christine stand and guided her toward his van. Apparently, Christine planned to stay the night again at Susan's, as Zach was on near-constant duty up at the Bistro, and Christine needed bedrest assistance. Christine, who'd been nothing if not completely self-sufficient for around forty years, clearly resented needing so much help all the time. Probably, this had contributed to her fears around motherhood and if she was cut out for it. Audrey gave her a final nod before Christine escaped into the chill of the mid-December night, knowing that their heavy conversation about their separate debacles had only just begun. This was the way of Christine and Audrey. Perhaps it always would be.

Lola collapsed on the couch alongside Amanda and Audrey to sip the last of her wine. She rubbed the top of Audrey's back lovingly and said, "It was so much fun to road trip with you all the way from Pennsylvania. And so good to have you back!"

"I wish we could steal her for good from Penn State," Amanda admitted.

Audrey curled a blanket over her shoulders and tried to make herself look very small. Sam stepped out from the kitchen with a Christmas cookie in hand and told Amanda that he needed to get going pretty soon. His eyes seemed wounded, as though he longed to ask her to come home with him but wasn't entirely sure where the line was between them. Amanda leaped up to walk him to the back door.

"Hey babe," Lola greeted Tommy, who adjusted his baseball cap in the corner like a fidgeting, tired child. "You about ready to get going?"

Tommy looked as though Lola had given him the greatest gift. "If you are," he replied sheepishly.

"I think that means we're out of here," Lola said. "Willa? You want someone to walk you back to Susan's?"

Willa blinked those strange, empty eyes across the living room, where she remained stationed at the chair by the bay window. She seemed captivated with the fluttering snow outside, which swept across the window, playing a stark contrast to the further, impenetrable darkness.

"I'd like to sit right here a little while longer if that's okay," Willa replied softly.

"I can walk her later," Audrey said. "I don't mind."

Lola arched an eyebrow toward Audrey, seemingly trying to come up with some way to resist this. After a strange moment's pause, however, Tommy appeared in the living room with Lola's coat in hand.

"I'll text you later," Lola said. "And see you tomorrow, probably."

"Get home safe," Audrey said. "I love you."

"Love you, too, Green Bean," Lola said before she ducked out into the impenetrable night.

With Grandpa Wes already tucked away in bed, and Amanda off with Sam somewhere, and Aunt Kerry back at home with Uncle Trevor— Audrey found herself face-to-face with her grandmother's long-lost little sister, Willa. In the silence that filled the room, Audrey was allowed time to gaze at this beautiful woman, whose features resembled those of Lola, Christine, and Susan, but still made up a glorious ensemble that seemed all Willa's own. Seated there at the bay window, this woman didn't look like a woman plagued with psychosis. Rather, she just looked worn down by the reality of her own existence. That and she seemed incredibly lonely.

Audrey recognized loneliness now, especially as she had spent the past few months at Penn State stewing in that very emotion, day-in and day-out.

"How are you finding it?" Audrey heard herself ask. "Being on the island after all this time away?"

Willa's cheek twitched as she gently turned her head toward Audrey's. She looked at her curiously and then allowed her lips to spread out into an enormous smile.

"You look the most like her, maybe," Willa said finally.

Audrey's cheeks burned. She stuttered, searching for something to say.

"I don't mean to make you nervous," Willa told her then. "I'm not that confused that I don't know where I am. I even know what year it is, if you can believe it."

"That's something I struggle with all the time," Audrey said, trying out a joke. "I never know what day of the week it is. Or my age. Am I twenty? Seventeen? Eleven? Time seems to just fly forward without rhyme or reason."

Willa's smile remained captivated. "You're funnier than she was, though. There's something very charming about you."

"I've always wanted to meet her," Audrey admitted thoughtfully. "When I see her photographs, I definitely feel like I'm looking at a black-and-white mirror."

Willa's smile waned for a moment as she folded and unfolded her hands across her lap. "I know that I learned she died, but the events around it are so fuzzy. 1997... My mother was dead by then, but my father... Well, I don't think we made it to the funeral. I asked your mother if she remembered me there, and she said no."

"Mom was only eleven," Audrey pointed out. "It's possible you were there. Maybe she doesn't remember."

"It seems wild to me that I can't remember these huge gaps of time..." Willa clucked her tongue.

Audrey placed her teeth on her lower lip, feeling despondent. Willa seemed a creature from another world. Audrey remembered reading about psychosis in one of her university textbooks sometime in September— something about Zelda Fitzgerald, the wife of F. Scott Fitzgerald, who'd suffered from psychosis but had spanned all levels of human emotion, from intense sorrow to the euphoria of the 1920s. Psychosis had seemed the price she had to pay to be one of the most fascinating and tragic creatures of the twentieth century. Almost assuredly, the pain hadn't fully been worth it.

Did this woman, Willa, before her span such heights of emotion?

"When you first arrived, what year did you think it was?" Audrey asked softly.

Willa pressed her lips together timidly. For a long moment, Audrey thought Willa hadn't heard her question at all.

"It seemed so clear to me that Anna would be at the Sunrise Cove Inn. It was where I left her when we moved away. Seemed that she should be safe there forever, waiting for me to return." Willa looked out in the distance again when she finished her words.

"It sounds like you got caught in a time warp," Audrey suggested.

"Something like that." Willa dropped her head back, extending her gorgeous, porcelain neck. "Before Mom kicked Anna out of the house, Anna and I had such beautiful times together. I remember once, I was riding my bike down the road and crashed it. I had cut my knee terribly and there was blood everywhere. Mom was home drunk and just not capable of caring for me at the time. Anna scooped me up and cleaned the wound and then asked Wes to drive us all to the apple orchard outside of Edgartown. My gosh, it was magical. I suppose now it was just a way for Anna to keep me away from Mom. But I wouldn't have been able to say that, then.

"Wes, Anna, and I spent the whole afternoon together, picking apples and eating apple pie slathered with too much whipped cream. I was captivated with Wes and Anna and wondered if I would ever feel something like that in my life, whatever it was these teenagers felt for one another. It seemed Anna had learned some sort of secret about the universe. I prayed she would teach it to me, too."

Immediately after this story, Willa's eyes widened. "I haven't thought of that story in years," she admitted. "It must be because I'm back here. I'm back on the Vineyard. It's like all the ghosts I've hidden from myself have been released."

Silence brewed between them. Willa pressed her palms together, on the verge of tears.

"Where did you and your parents move?" Audrey asked.

"Just outside of Boston," Willa replied, still staring out into the distance.

"Nice. I grew up in Boston, too," Audrey told her.

Willa's eyes grew cloudy with confusion. Audrey realized she didn't want to cover every little piece of family history about why she, Lola, Susan, and Christine had spent so much time away from the Vineyard. It was far too complicated to explain.

"Did you stay in Boston after high school?" Audrey asked.

"I did," Willa said as she furrowed her brow. It seemed that just then, she built a wall between herself and Audrey.

"And did you go to college?" Audrey asked, wanting to dig a bit deeper.

"I don't— I mean. I don't..." Willa shook her head and placed her fingers at her temples. "There are so many gaps like I said."

Just then, the back door screeched open to reveal Susan, who had rushed back through the billowing snow.

"Hi, you two," Susan greeted brightly. "Are you getting to know each other?"

Audrey's nostrils flared. She had felt on the verge of discovering some sort of truth behind Willa's sudden, mysterious return.

"I'd really like to get some sleep," Willa told Susan then. "That is, if you don't mind."

"Of course. I came back to check on you for that very reason," Susan said brightly. "I put your coat, gloves, and hat right back here."

Susan burrowed herself back in the mudroom as Willa stood. Her posture was regal and her chin high. Audrey stood as well as her heart thumped away in her throat. It was difficult, truly, to imagine this woman as a young girl, dancing through the apple trees with previous versions of Grandpa Wes and Grandma Anna. Still, this captured memory— this vision that nobody else in the family knew about, warmed Audrey from the inside.

"Good night, Willa," Audrey said as Willa slipped on her puffy coat. "I hope to talk to you soon."

Susan glanced Audrey's way with heavy curiosity.

"She looked just like her when she left," Willa said softly, mostly to herself. "She's like the last image I ever had of my big sister."

Susan's smile waned as fear took hold. "Let's get you back home, Willa. I'm sure Audrey will come over for breakfast in the morning. She's never one to miss a good meal."

Audrey lifted a hand and waved her fingers gently as Willa and Susan stepped out into the night. Curiosity took hold of her, planting its seed and threatening to blossom. What on earth had Willa been up to all these years? And what had caused this strange psychosis? Audrey burned with the desire to figure it out.

Chapter Eleven

On the morning of December 14th, the door to the guest bedroom at Susan's home squeaked open to allow for tentative quiet footfalls. Christine, nestled away under multiple comforters yet with her toes poked out on the far end of the blanket, opened her eyes gently, feeling a part of a dream. There before her stood Zach Walters, with a bouquet of roses lifted and his smile bright.

"Good morning, beautiful," he murmured in a sultry voice.

Christine positioned her elbows beneath her to prop herself up. She blinked, trying to wash away her confusion. "What are you doing here? I thought you had to open the Bistro?"

"The holiday chef I hired said she could start work a little bit earlier," Zach replied. "I told her about your bedrest and our baby, and she pounced on me. She asked me why the heck I wasn't at home with my pregnant girlfriend. I told her I was the biggest idiot in the world."

Zach placed the bouquet of roses gently on the bedside table and shifted onto the edge of the bed. Christine lifted her chin and closed her eyes as his pillow-soft lips came over hers and his hand stretched across her stomach.

"I planned a day for just the two of us," Zach breathed as he drew a strand of hair around her ear.

"You didn't have to do that," Christine whispered.

"I wanted to," Zach replied tenderly. "We only have so much time together, just the two of us, especially now that Audrey's back with her son. I want us to enjoy it."

Christine felt languid and joyful, as though time itself had finally stopped short and allowed her a moment of peace. Zach assisted her through the living room and back out to his van, where he strapped her in delicately, telling her about how her cat had stationed itself at the front door night-after-night, meowing for her.

"He'll be happy to see you, that's for sure," Zach said. "I just don't cut it."

"We've been through a lot together," Christine told him as a smile curved toward both ears.

"And there's a whole lot more where that came from."

Back at home, Zach drew Christine a warm bubble bath while he set to work on breakfast. He left the door open between the bathroom and the hallway that led to the kitchen, which allowed Christine to enjoy the beautiful soundtrack of his life's work—the sizzle of the skillet, the chop of the knife against the onions, and the occasional, "Oh, Christine, I've outdone myself here," which he often had to call out when he was particularly excited about a new recipe.

All the while, Christine felt herself fall into a meditative state. The anxiety that had welled up within her over the previous month fell back. She could still sense the fears, but they seemed somewhere in the distance as her arms and legs floated, weightless, in the bath.

Years ago, back in Manhattan, she'd been a frequent bath-taker. Usually, she'd taken to the bath during a particularly depressive spell, often with a cocktail or glass of wine beside her as she allowed her psyche to fall back from her self-hatred and goop into drunkenness.

Since her return to the Vineyard, that sort of escape hadn't been possible. Her drinking had subsided greatly until her pregnancy when she'd cut it off entirely. Now, her mind seemed equipped to handle the intricacies of its own fears without the clouding of alcohol.

When she'd seen Audrey suck down that glass of wine after her coming-home dinner party a few nights before, Christine had recognized something sinister behind it. Audrey wanted to escape from something within herself. She had no idea what it could be.

Zach returned to the bathroom to assist Christine into a fluffy white robe. He then guided her to her "throne," the living room couch, where he'd set up a beautiful breakfast tray, complete with Eggs Benedict and roasted garlic breakfast potatoes and tart orange juice. The large living room window presented a picture-perfect winter wonderland, and even her cat, Felix, sat in the windowsill, peering out curiously.

"So quiet around here without Max," Christine said softly.

"I miss him," Zach admitted. "But not enough to call Audrey to bring him back right now."

Christine laughed good-naturedly as she sliced through the Eggs Benedict. She and Zach fell into a comfortable silence as the snow fluttered outside, enveloping them.

Mid-way through his meal, Zach placed his fork and knife back on his plate with a soft clank, then folded his hands across his lap.

"I've never seen you stop eating halfway through a meal," Christine teased.

Zach's smile was infectious. "Now that I've finally had some moments to myself, away from the Bistro, I've found time to think." He reached over and laced his fingers through Christine's. "This is about to be one of the greatest adventures of our lives. And I feel so privileged, Christine, that I get to embark on that adventure with you. I know I've been an imperfect partner in the past. No doubt that I'll be an imperfect partner in the future, as well. But I just want you and our baby to know that I'll be there, through thick and thin, imperfectly, until the day I die."

Christine's eyes welled with tears. She placed her teeth over the top of her bottom lip as she stuttered her response.

"Until this morning, I've stirred with so many fears around the next few weeks," Christine murmured. "Those Braxton Hicks contractions terrified me. All I could think, during each contraction, was, 'Oh my gosh, I'm not ready! We're not ready! It's not time!' But sitting here with you, with the snow falling down outside... I can feel, now, that every decision I've made in the past has led me to you, to this family we're building. I'm so grateful."

Zach spread a hand over the top of Christine's back and rubbed it gently. She placed her head on his chest and exhaled all the air from her lungs.

"I've been going over my notes from the childbirth class," Zach said then.

"You took notes?" Christine asked, her heart lifting.

"Oh gosh, yes. Those classes were so jam-packed with information that I wrote everything out after the fact," Zach said.

Christine's heart welled with gladness as Zach began to game-plan the upcoming labor and delivery, as though it was just another frantic night at the Bistro. As a head chef, he was no stranger to chaos and stress— and he knew how to orchestrate the world around him to build beautiful experiences. He'd read about a number of other elements to put in the overnight bag for the hospital and even suggested that they buy a few extra things she hadn't thought of for the baby's nursery. She nestled into the sound of his deep, textured voice and nourished herself with the nutritionally-vibrant food he'd created for them both. In the corner, the Christmas tree's lights twinkled expectantly. It was only eleven days till Christmas.

Chapter Twelve

Max's little lips curled around the top of the bottle before he latched powerfully and began to gulp down his milk. The once-teensy baby had grown enormously, especially in Audrey's eyes, as she'd missed so much. As he ate, she tipped her fingers across his seemingly large toes, which wiggled at her touch, and she stroked his chunky calves and arms as her heart tried to choose between stress at the passage of time and gladness that her baby was plump and healthy.

Grandpa Wes entered the living room to find Audrey seated on the floor, her back against the couch, Max in her arms. He grinned at her sheepishly, like a mischievous teenager, and then pressed his finger against his lips.

"Do you know what I found?" he whispered.

"What?" Audrey asked.

Grandpa Wes's knees creaked as he bent low to grip a Tupperware container on the lowest shelf of the kitchen cabinet. He then ripped off the top to reveal an entire container of Buckeye Christmas cookies, a treasure trove.

"I thought Amanda told us that we were out of them!" Audrey gasped.

"I'm pretty sure that Amanda lied to save our waistlines..." Grandpa Wes clucked his tongue.

"That is so typical Amanda," Audrey blurted. "Remember all those months last year when she tried to get us to eat salads for lunch?"

"I've never fully recovered," Grandpa Wes affirmed. He placed a napkin on the couch to the left of Audrey's head, on which he planted the Buckeye for a post-feeding snack. "Guessing he'll be out like a light after that big bottle."

"That's the hope," Audrey said.

Grandpa Wes's dark grey eyebrows dropped low. He dug his teeth into the Buckeye as he studied Audrey and little Max.

"It's really nice to have you back here, Audrey," he said. "When you left, a little light left with you."

Audrey tried to drum up a smile as she met her grandfather's eyes. But before she could, her phone buzzed at the far end of her leg. Max's surprise at the sound made him unclench his lips and let out a wild wail until Audrey coaxed him back to the bottle once more.

The phone buzz was an email alert. Audrey puffed out her cheeks as she lifted the phone toward her eyes, even as Max continued to eat. Grandpa Wes settled across the living room, a crossword puzzle stretched out before him on the top of a book and a pen settled gently in his right hand.

The email read: **AUDREY SHERIDAN - SEMESTER GRADES**

Audrey couldn't envision a worse time to receive this message. Here, with her baby son across her lap, in the cozy ecosystem of the Sheridan house, at the edge of the Vineyard Sound— here she would learn the fate of her horrific semester. She tapped the link and was flung through the internet portal, all the way to the university website's grade listings.

And there, alongside her name, was a smattering of Cs, Bs, and a single A, in Creative Writing. The final exam that she'd missed had knocked her grade from a B+ to a C-, which dragged her GPA all the way down to a gut-wrenching 2.52.

This wasn't the sort of grade that gave Audrey any sort of excitement for her future in journalism. It wouldn't excite her future employers either— if she had any to look forward to at all.

Max finished his bottle and smacked his palms together excitedly before suddenly, just as Grandpa Wes had predicted, his arms fell on either side of him and his eyelids closed. Audrey placed the bottle next to the couch and lifted her son against her chest as her heart ballooned.

"Are you okay, Audrey?" Grandpa Wes asked as she stood up on shaky legs.

"Oh? Yes. I'm fine." The words came out in stuttered syllables.

Grandpa Wes dropped his pen against his crossword puzzle and gazed at her knowingly, as though he could see all the way through her. Audrey quickly made her way toward the staircase to avoid any probing questions, then headed upstairs to place Max in his crib.

Perhaps this failure was for the best.

Perhaps this meant that she could raise Max the way she always wanted to.

Perhaps this meant she would return to her position right there at the house, teasing her Grandpa Wes and picking fun at Amanda.

Perhaps.

It was difficult not to feel like the greatest-possible failure, especially since she'd outlined her plans to her family with such affirmation. Beyond anything, she'd learned never to count her chickens before they hatched. Not again.

A few hours later, after Max arose from his mid-afternoon nap, Amanda arrived back from her shift at the downtown Oak Bluffs law offices and headed upstairs to coax Audrey out of her funk.

"You've been wearing those pajamas for three days straight," Amanda pointed out, a carrot stick lifted. "Why don't we go to Cousin Kelli's boutique? Try on some second-hand clothes? I've been dying for something new. I'm so tired of all these business-appropriate clothes I've worn all year long."

Audrey grumbled inwardly, but soon found herself in the steam of the shower, scrubbing her tired skin and tearing through the tangles in her hair with a wet brush. When she appeared downstairs to find Grandpa Wes, Amanda, and Max around another platter of vegetables, Amanda said, "Okay. That'll do," as though Audrey needed to pass some sort of test.

"Too bad we're out of those Buckeyes, huh?" Grandpa Wes said as Audrey and Amanda donned their coats and prepared little Max in his carrier.

"It really is," Amanda returned in a sing-song voice. "But I'm sure we'll have more for Christmas Day."

Grandpa Wes and Audrey made heavy eye contact as Audrey cut her teeth over her lower lip and struggled not to laugh.

"I sure hope so," Grandpa Wes said.

Up at Kelli's boutique, Max flew a hand through his little hanging toys in his carrier, his eyes toward the ceiling, as Amanda and Audrey scuttled through countless vintage sweaters, skirts, jeans from the nineties, and dresses from the seventies. The sound system blared old hits from the nineties and two-thousands, hitting on Britney Spears and Christina Aguilera, songs that made both Audrey and Amanda howl in the dressing rooms.

"You two should really start a band," Kelli quipped as she stepped out from behind the cash register's iPad set-up and beamed at them, with ten hangers hanging from her outstretched finger.

"We know," Audrey replied, her heart lighter than it had been in hours. "We've decided to practice here if that's okay for you?"

"Absolutely," Kelli returned with a smile. "As long as you let me join."

"It's a deal." Amanda jumped out of the dressing room in a long-sleeved, long-panted onesie, bright-orange in coloring, with flared pants.

"Amanda..." Audrey teased. "Are you trying to time travel?"

"What do you think Sam would think of it?" Amanda asked as she shifted left, then right in the reflection of the mirror.

"I think he would say, I didn't know I was dating Donna from That *70's Show*," Audrey countered.

"Donna's hot," Amanda affirmed. She then yanked her head around to glare at Audrey playfully. "And besides, who said Sam and me are dating?"

"I don't know. Maybe the fact that you guys spend every waking moment together," Audrey stated with a shrug.

Amanda's grimace soon flourished into a smile. She swept her hair back behind her shoulders and heaved a sigh. "You're right. It's a little too weird for me."

"Finally, she listens to reason," Audrey said to Kelli, who burst into laughter.

A little over an hour later, with three stuffed bags of vintage goods in Amanda's hand and Max's carrier in Audrey's, the Sheridan cousins stepped into the soft grey light of the late afternoon. Audrey still hadn't fessed up the news of her grades and carried it around like a knife through the stomach. She half-expected Amanda to call her out on it, but she seemed deep in her own thoughts, presumably regarding her budding love for Sam.

Amanda had parked the car toward the corner, alongside a ten-foot-tall, fully-decorated Christmas tree, which glittered with bright blue Christmas bulbs. As she hunted for her keys in her pockets, smashing her sides, Max let out a wail.

"Oh, honey. It's okay! We're almost home. And Aunt Amanda hasn't lost the keys, I promise," Audrey murmured in a sing-song voice.

"Ha," Amanda said.

"Audrey?"

The voice rang out from about eight feet away. Audrey yanked her head up to find a six-foot-three figure, his facial features dim and inarticulate in the late-afternoon December light. She would have recognized that voice anywhere, though. She'd heard it time and time again, through her cell, as he'd called her during her panicked studying nights the previous semester if only to assure her that everything would be all right.

This wasn't the time to tell him that everything hadn't turned out so great.

"Oh. Noah..." Audrey shook her head violently and lifted her chin to meet his eyes. Max seemed to sense the anxiety in her heart and finally calmed down.

Noah stepped closer, bringing himself into the light of the street lamp. Beside him, a twenty-something woman stood in a periwinkle coat and a pair of heeled knee-high boots. Her auburn hair was cropped toward her ears, and her green eyes were bright and intelligent. Audrey could have melted on the sidewalk as she took in the sight before her.

"When did you get back?" Noah asked, trying to keep his voice upbeat.

"Just a few days ago," Audrey told him, careful not to glance in the direction of this mystery girl.

"Well, that's great. Welcome," Noah replied. "Although I'm sure, knowing your future plans, you won't be on the island for long."

"We'll see," Audrey returned.

Looking at Noah seemed like looking too long at the sun. Pain rocketed through her heart. She suddenly stepped back, grabbed the back door handle of Amanda's vehicle, and opened it almost too quickly. Later, Amanda would comment that Audrey had "tried to take the car door off the car."

"We'd better get going," Audrey suggested. "Max is crazy-hungry. Actually, I am too, which, as you might remember, if I don't get food, I turn really quick."

Noah laughed nervously. "I hope you have some Reese's Pieces squirreled away in there."

Audrey's pain was now insurmountable. This was how they'd first met. He had purchased the candies for her in the NICU as she'd watched her baby struggle through the first weeks of his life.

"That would be helpful, but I highly doubt there's any,"

Audrey said hurriedly. She then forced herself to look at this strange, beautiful girl and say, "It was good to see you." She then buckled Max's carrier into the back and flung herself into the front, as Amanda hustled around to the driver's side and followed suit.

Once they were out on the road, Audrey exhaled all the air from her lungs and pressed her chin against her chest.

"Are you okay?" Amanda finally asked. They were the first words either of them had spoken since their mad dash away from Noah.

"God, that was awful. Much worse than I'd imagined in my mind," Audrey murmured.

Amanda heaved a sigh. Up ahead, the green light shifted to yellow, and Amanda eased a foot over the brake. Neither of them seemed to know what to say.

"Do you know who that girl is?" Audrey finally asked.

"I've never seen her before," Amanda said.

"She's pretty," Audrey offered.

"She's okay."

"You have to say that, legally," Audrey teased, despite the darkness within her heart.

Amanda groaned. "Come on, Audrey. You were the one who never knew what you wanted with Noah. You strung him along until you finally ended it. You can't blame him for moving on."

Audrey dropped her head against the car seat as her heart hammered. "I know that."

"I mean, for the record, Noah looked at you just then like you were the only woman in the world," Amanda said pointedly. "I'm sure whoever that girl is, she's giving him the cold shoulder right now."

Audrey let out a single laugh. "I don't know."

"Seriously," Amanda returned. "If I was that girl, I would not go home with that guy tonight. He has another priority and that priority's name is Audrey Sheridan."

Chapter Thirteen

"There she is. Our runaway." Susan greeted Christine lovingly as Zach helped her through the doorway of the Sheridan house for the first time in several days. She kicked off her snow-lined boots in the mudroom and fell into Susan's arms as the others called out "hellos" from the living room and kitchen. Deeper in the house, sinful smells of baking cookies and spiced wines swelled.

"I told Zach I needed sister time," Christine told her as she shifted slowly toward the couch.

"And I need some time for Christmas shopping," Zach said brightly. He followed after Christine and helped her situate herself on the couch, then pressed a delicate kiss on her lips. "I'll see you later," he whispered, his eyes aglow.

After Zach closed the door behind him and drove his van safely down the gravel-lined driveway, Susan sat across from Christine on the couch, nibbled a Christmas cookie and said, "You two seem awfully in love."

"They're nesting," Lola teased from the kitchen. "It's disgusting."

"And beautiful," Amanda countered from her stance on the ground, where little Max bobbed around on all fours.

"Where's Audrey?" Christine asked.

Audrey peeked her head around the corner, where she sat at the dining room table across from a silent Willa. "We're doing the crossword in here," she called. "Grandpa just went in for a nap."

"What a cozy little place," Christine said.

"All we do is eat, sleep, and gossip," Susan returned.

A few minutes later, Audrey stood from the dining room table and announced that she and Willa wanted to take a walk through the woods. Willa's eyes seemed clear, despite her commitment to secrecy about why she'd come. She seemed almost latched to Audrey, following after her like a little lost dog.

"You're okay with Max a little while longer?" Audrey asked Amanda as she settled a winter hat over her head.

"Sure thing, honey," Amanda said. "Me and Max are good pals by now."

The bright red of Audrey's coat soon disappeared between the trees that lined the Sheridan and Frampton grounds. Christine took a small bite from a bell-shaped Christmas cookie.

"I just got back from another psychiatric appointment with Willa," Lola muttered, as though Willa, all the way in the wintery woods, could still hear.

"And?" Christine asked.

Lola shook her head. "Not much. She seems clear on several points thus far. First off, she came here to look for our mother, who, it seems, left her in a very sad situation when she married Dad. The doctor says it's possible that she generated this psychosis due to memories from that era... From her alcoholic parents and how lonely she was at the time. But it's also not very likely."

"Audrey thinks there's something else at play," Susan said.

"Audrey has started to do a bit of digging surrounding Willa and her life before she reached the island," Lola added.

"Sounds like that is up her alley," Christine replied. "All that work at journalism school."

Amanda nodded firmly. "There aren't a whole lot of clues about her right now. She wears no wedding ring, for one."

"And for another, when the doctor asked her what her street address and phone number were, she had no idea," Lola said. "But she could remember her street address and phone number from her childhood before she left the island."

"When she arrived, she even used her maiden name when she spoke to Sam at the Sunrise Cove," Lola stated as a matter of fact.

"It's like many decades of her life have just been completely ripped from her mind," Amanda said.

"It's just strange that she came back here for some kind of solace." Susan tucked a strand of hair behind her ear before continuing. "After knowing this place only as the dark home with cruel parents."

"But I think her actions thus far show something else," Lola suggested. "They show how much she loved our mother. Which..." She pressed a hand over her heart. "It just breaks my heart to know that."

The three Sheridan Sisters held the silence for a long moment as Max, Anna Sheridan's great-grandson, scrambled across the rug that Anna Sheridan herself had stitched together. Every nook and cranny of that very house seemed edged with the memory of Anna Sheridan.

Now, Willa had arrived to soak up that memory.

"She's started to lighten up a bit," Susan said. "She helps me around the kitchen here and there and talks to Kellan about his homework assignments. She seems very knowledgeable about a number of things. It's just hard to fill in the gaps. What happened between the moment she and her parents left the Vineyard— and her arrival back just a week and a half ago?"

Twenty minutes later, Audrey and Willa's laughter erupted through the back door as they stomped their boots of snow and lined them along the far wall.

"And she told me that my snowman looked just like a football," Willa said, sputtering with giggles.

"She didn't! That's so mean!" Audrey cried.

"What are you two on about?" Lola's eyes shone with curiosity.

"Willa's just telling me a story about her and Anna," Audrey explained.

Willa stepped down the hallway and snapped her fingers. "It's strange. These thoughts just keep coming back to me as I spend more time with Audrey."

"I've started to write them down," Audrey said as she grabbed her notebook from the table next to the couch and flipped through.

Susan, Christine, and Lola gaped hungrily at Audrey and Willa.

"You've got stories about Mom in there?" Lola breathed.

Audrey nodded as she scribbled this new snowman memory into the notebook. "I figured it was good to piece together what Willa remembered so far, especially as the medication works its magic."

Lola beckoned for the notebook, which Audrey eventually passed toward her. Susan leaped to stand behind Lola as she flipped through the little stories, which illustrated the small, day-to-day memories that had come to Willa since her arrival.

Willa collapsed in the chair by the bay window and rubbed her palms together tenderly. Her eyes caught the wild blue of the Vineyard Sound and seemed more illuminated than those first few days of confusion.

"This apple orchard story." Lola breathed. "Anna and Dad took Willa to pick apples to keep Willa out of the house." Her eyes glittered with tears as she lifted her chin toward Audrey. Her voice lowered as she added, "But still no sense for what happened after the Vineyard?"

"Nothing," Audrey admitted. "But I'm digging into the rest. It might take some time."

Lola and Susan exchanged worried glances. Lola then grabbed a Kleenex from the table and dabbed the corners of her eyes. Outside, clouds rolled lower and then opened to spill out dramatic, fluffy snowflakes. Willa, who now sipped her tea and continued to gaze out, wordless, seemed captivated. What was it like, Christine wondered now, to remember so much of your past without any understanding of the current context of your life?

A few hours later, Lola dressed to meet Tommy and his ex-stepfather, Stan, who'd spent the majority of the past few months as a resident at the Katama Lodge and Wellness Spa. The enormous lodge on the south-eastern coast of the island was a much-sought-after space for women across the country on the lookout for healing and wellness. Stan had gotten wrapped up in it all when he'd saved some of the head workers of the spa from certain disaster during the recent Hurricane Janine. As the hurricane had destroyed much of his house, he'd needed a place to stay and the Lodge had been there for him.

As Stan was a man who'd spent the majority of his life as an outsider after his involvement in the death of Anna Sheridan, Christine had to imagine he felt nothing if not relief for this fresh start.

A warm bed. A listening ear. A bright morning.

These things were medicine.

Susan soon headed back to her place to check on Scott and Kellan, who "couldn't make a proper dinner to save their lives," while Audrey and Amanda headed upstairs with Max to gossip and try on their new clothes from Kelli's boutique. This left Willa and Christine alone in the cozy living room, both wordless and stewing in their own thoughts.

"I suppose I'd better text Zach to come to get me," Christine said earnestly, surprising herself with having to fill the silence between herself and this relative stranger.

Willa's eyes widened then dropped toward Christine's stomach, which swelled beneath the knitted blanket. She stood and walked slowly toward Christine's couch, then sat at the far end, near Christine's feet. Normally, this was an intimate space reserved only for Susan or Lola or Audrey.

With Willa there, however, Christine felt oddly closer to her, despite their lack of previous conversation.

"You really look so beautiful," Willa said softly.

Christine's lips parted in surprise. "Thank you. I don't really feel like it."

"I can imagine," Willa murmured. "But it's, well. I really longed for a child. For years and years, I think." Her eyes grew clouded as she struggled with the feeling.

Christine furrowed her brow, unsure of what to say. How could she translate that she'd longed for a child, too, only to receive this miracle baby as a sort of gift from the universe?

"I just hate that my brain isn't working," Willa breathed. "I sit here with Anna Sheridan's daughters and pinch myself, wanting only to know you and ask you questions and laugh with you. But my tongue is inarticulate. I can't think of a single question. And I find these precious moments pass me by as I stir in my own anxiety."

Christine reached across her legs and took Willa's hand in hers. The intimacy of this moment swelled around them.

"You're going to figure it out, Aunt Willa," Christine murmured. "We're going to help you."

"You've already helped so much," Willa whispered. "I just can't really figure out why."

Christine's throat tightened. "I suppose it's because none of us were really put-together before our return to the Vineyard, either. We went off to all corners of the east coast— Boston, Newark, and New York City, and we avoided one another, as our memories felt too painful to face."

Willa's lips parted in surprise. "I had no idea."

"No. I suppose you wouldn't be able to see it, spending time with us now," Christine returned. "But when I arrived here only a year and a half ago, I was a much different, much more unhappy person. I have my sisters, Audrey, Amanda, and of course, my father, to thank for that."

Willa set her jaw determinedly. "That gives me hope, Christine. Thank you. Really, thank you."

Chapter Fourteen

EMAIL SUBJECT: **Audrey Sheridan - Semester Grades**

Hi, Audrey.

I'm sure it's not your favorite thing, being checked up on like this, but as I haven't heard from you since my previous email, here I am again.

I know you've had a difficult semester, Audrey. You told me that you wanted to come back to Penn State in pursuit of your journalism degree in order to prove it to yourself and your son that you could make it in the field that you've dreamed of. I know that your mother is a renowned journalist in her own right— and assuredly, you've got a whole lot of her gumption and talent.

With that said, I've had a talk with a number of your professors and had a look at your grades. Unfortunately, at this time, these grades are not sufficient to remain in journalism school. Your professors find you to be intelligent and diligent but distracted.

If your grades rise over the next two semesters, it's possible that you can re-apply to the journalism school.

I would still be available to be your school counselor throughout this in-between time. Perhaps we could have a video conference to decide which classes would suit you best next semester.

I hope to hear from you soon, Audrey.

Merry Christmas.

Ms. Evans

Audrey sat at the edge of her mother's childhood bed with tears streaming down her cheeks. She re-read the email then threw her phone on the mattress as her body shook with rage. This was it: the final nail in the coffin. There was nothing else she could do.

Max cooed at her from his crib, seemingly trying to boost her mood. Audrey lifted from the mattress and tip-toed, barefoot, across the room, where she stood over Max, her hands gripping the edge of the crib.

"Why are you so good to me?" she asked Max softly. "I don't deserve it."

Max buzzed his lips, and Audrey erupted with laughter, as though he was the very best comedian, better still than any twenty-something male attempting the comedy scene. Audrey bent down and lifted his warm little body against her as her tears dried. There was no use crying over spilled milk. There would be enough spilled milk in her future. That was sure.

With easy motions and a vibrant smile, despite the pain within her heart, Audrey changed her baby and then headed downstairs with him to heat up a bottle. There, she found her mother, Susan,

Willa, and Grandpa Wes around the dining room table, feasting on Frosted Delights donuts like there was no tomorrow.

Audrey's heart warmed still more at the sight of them. These people loved her, C- grade and all. If she'd gotten an F? They would have wrapped their arms around her, stuffed her with baked goods, and said, *"There will be good luck on the way."* She just wasn't sure she wanted to fess up quite yet.

"Good morning, everyone," Audrey greeted them brightly.

"Morning!" Grandpa Wes returned as he lifted a donut in greeting. "You wouldn't believe it, but they have a whole new Christmas flavor. Peppermint."

"Is that even legal?" Audrey asked.

"The jury's still out," Susan teased.

Willa laughed good-naturedly as she selected her own chocolate-frosted donut.

"What's all this?" Audrey asked, pointing at the wide selection of photographs between Willa, Susan, and Grandpa Wes.

"We found them in a shoebox upstairs," Susan said. "Photos Mom still had from when Willa was a little girl."

Audrey inspected the photos as Max smacked his lips in her ear. There Willa stood, maybe six or seven, frequently with scraped knees and pigtails. In a few, Anna wore what seemed to be a prom dress or a homecoming dress as she bent low to position her face alongside her sister's. Willa, sometimes with big gaps between her teeth, beamed out from the photographs, her love for her sister unquestioned.

"Look at you, Aunt Willa!" Audrey beamed.

Willa blushed. "I just couldn't keep those teeth in my head, could I?"

"If I remember it right, you were overjoyed each time they fell out," Wes said. "You asked me to tie a string to one of your front teeth and tear it out."

Willa shrieked with laughter. "That sounds about right. I was always hoping to grow up a little bit faster. Now, gosh, how I wish I could turn back time."

Audrey prepared a bottle and sat with Max on the couch while the others continued to pore over the photographs. Willa offered various tales here and there— about her initial memories of Wes or when Anna had taken her for a hike at the Aquinnah Cliffs. Susan listened with her head bent low, as though Willa translated the most important facts of Anna's life.

"I hate to do this," Susan breathed about fifteen minutes later, "But I have to head into work. I have a few clients to meet before we dig into the holiday season completely."

"That's too bad," Grandpa Wes said.

"Kellan said something about going out birdwatching with you this morning?" Susan asked.

"Did he?" Grandpa Wes said.

"I'll text him real quick and get him over here," Susan assured him. "He's had a few days of Christmas break, and I don't think he's spent a single day not playing those silly video games."

By the time eleven o'clock rolled around, Willa, Audrey, and Max were the only remaining family members in the warm cocoon of the Sheridan house. Audrey placed Max delicately in his carrier as he slept, his belly full from the bottle, while Willa flipped through the photos from her youth yet again.

"I haven't seen these before," Willa admitted as Audrey walked past, on the hunt for a donut. "I suppose Anna took them and tucked them away. All those years, I thought maybe she didn't care for me any longer. More likely was that she wrote me letters that my mother and father didn't allow me to see."

"They sound like terribly cruel people, Willa. I'm so sorry," Audrey whispered, her voice rasping.

Willa shook her head as her eyes grew clouded. "It's no good to blame the dead, I suppose."

Audrey wasn't sure what to say. She stepped back into the kitchen to brew herself a cup of tea as Willa remained at the table. Through the little window that peered out from the kitchen to the dining room, Audrey watched as Willa flipped photographs back and forth, studying the dates Anna had written on the back.

Throughout so much of her life, Audrey had kept diaries diligently, scribing dates and times of her thoughts and feelings and opinions.

Since her arrival back to Penn State and away from her son, however, she'd lost the habit. Perhaps she hadn't wanted to look at her emotions too deeply. Perhaps it had felt like an inner storm.

As Audrey stood in the kitchen, her mug of tea lifted, Max awoke with a giant wail. Before Audrey could leap toward him to calm him, Willa rushed for him, drawing her hands beneath his little body and lifting him against her. She seemed a natural.

"Hey there, big boy," she whispered as she bobbed him gently, a hand across his upper back.

"You got him?" Audrey asked from the kitchen doorway, her forehead knotted with worry.

"I got him," Willa murmured, her eyes still toward Max, whose cries had subsided.

Audrey's heartbeat calmed for a moment as she took in the vision of this beautiful woman, a stand-in great-grandmother for

Baby Max. As she took a step back toward her mug on the kitchen counter, however, Willa lifted her eyes back toward Audrey's.

And at that moment, all of Audrey's blood drained from her face.

Willa's eyes were strange and faraway, as though she existed in another realm. She continued to bob Max, who cooed playfully, even as Willa blinked at Audrey with a mix of annoyance and fear.

"Has Harvey picked up the turkey yet?" Willa demanded, her voice harsh.

Audrey felt as though her stomach was filled with rocks. She stepped delicately toward her son, careful not to make any sudden motions.

"Well? Has he?" Willa asked.

Audrey pressed her lips together. How could she de-escalate this situation without causing harm?

"I think he has," she replied softly. "I think he's on his way home with the turkey."

Willa exhaled, seemingly relieved. "Gosh, he's worked so hard lately. That power plant's scheduling is all but killing them. And it's not like I want to complain. I know he puts food on the table. I know he cares for me more than he can say."

Harvey? Who was this Harvey? Audrey's throat felt terribly tight.

"Why don't you get started in the kitchen? I can take the baby," Audrey suggested softly.

"Harvey told me he'd quit. He said it plain as day," Willa continued, as though she hadn't heard her.

"I know he did," Audrey whispered, her voice catching.

"In what world should a husband lie to you?" Willa asked.

"Even if it's meant to keep you happy. When we married, I said for richer, for poorer. Didn't I? You were there."

Audrey blinked back tears as her fears escalated. Willa's shoulders fell forward as exhaustion took hold of her.

"He said he'd be back with the turkey," she breathed, mostly to Max, who cooed in response.

Suddenly, with the strength of a young mother who would do anything to protect her son, Audrey rushed forward and lifted Max from Willa's arms. The abrupt movement made Max wail with tears. The sound of it seemed to knock Willa out from her strange episode.

Willa flung her fingers across her cheeks and blinked at Audrey. Her eyes were lined with confusion. As Audrey bobbed Max against her, Willa collapsed in the chair by the bay window and gaped at the ground.

"My God..."

"Are you okay, Aunt Willa?" Audrey asked.

"Yes. Yes, I think so. Gosh, I felt my thoughts go a million other places. I felt myself so far away."

"Maybe we should call the ambulance," Audrey said.

"No. No. I don't want to go back to the hospital," Willa breathed. "Please. I promise. I won't do anything else. I'll go straight to Susan's place and put myself to bed."

Audrey closed her eyes tight as her thoughts swirled in circles. "Have you been taking your medication?"

"I have been," Willa said softly.

"And who... who is Harvey, Willa?"

Willa's lips parted with surprise. "Harvey. That name..." Her eyes grew clouded again. "It seems like someone from a dream."

Max giggled outright, as though Willa had just told the

funniest of all jokes. Audrey's heart felt squeezed with sorrow. Before she knew just what to say, Willa marched across the living room to collect her things in the mudroom.

"No, Willa. Please. Don't go over there and sit by yourself alone," Audrey pleaded softly. "Nobody should be alone. Not now. Not around Christmas."

Willa paused above her winter boots, her fingers stretched out like spiders' legs.

"You can take a nap in my bedroom if you want to," Audrey said. "But me and Max will be down here, waiting for you whenever you want to hang out again. Okay?"

Willa's chin wiggled back and forth with a certain heaviness. "You promise you don't want me out of here as soon as possible?"

"Aunt Willa..." Audrey was aghast. "You came all this way to the Vineyard for help. Now, let us help you. Please."

Chapter Fifteen

Audrey sat at the edge of the downstairs couch, her eyes alert as her brain raced through many states of panic and intrigue and fear. Max's chunky cheek pressed hard against her shoulder as he slept on, frequently pawing at her upper chest as though he searched for something within his dreams. Relief that Willa's strange psychosis hadn't in any way affected her son remained a powerful force.

Willa— who'd been on the hunt for Harvey with the turkey, presumably for some kind of Thanksgiving or Christmas celebration.

Who was this Harvey?

Audrey placed Max gently in his downstairs crib, grabbed her MacBook, and sat cross-legged at the dining room table with her fingers poised over the keyboard. A split second later, the memory of her journalism counselor's email returned to her mind. Apparently, she wasn't cut out to be a journalist.

Or was she? Hadn't she learned a thing or two at Penn State the previous semester, despite the aching sorrow she'd carried around with her?

Journalism was the search for the ultimate truth. A journalist had a responsibility to humanity, utilizing their intellect and their curiosity and their word-wisdom to craft a three-dimensional portrait of reality. Willa now lurked in the in-between of reality and non-reality. Her mind was poison, and she and the rest of the family suffered from it.

It was up to Audrey to set it straight.

The first few searches for Willa came up empty. She'd arrived on the island without any driver's license or form of identification, which made it difficult to know her last name or her place of address throughout her life. This last indication of a potential husband, though— that had the potential to lead to real results.

Approximately fifty-five minutes later, after a wild goose hunt down a Boston suburb's social media posting, Audrey stopped short at a photograph of a large group of people, all in their forties, fifties, and sixties. The photograph had been taken at this same Boston suburb's local golf course, where someone named Harvey Jackman had arranged a golf outing to raise money for children with cancer.

Audrey's eyes widened as she positioned her mouse from one face to another until she found Harvey Jackman tagged, center-stage in the photograph. He was a handsome man of maybe fifty-five, with broad shoulders and a healthy golfer's tan. He wore a striped turquoise shirt with a collar, and his left arm was wrapped around the beautiful woman beside him— his life partner, it seemed like.

Willa Jackman.

In the photograph, Willa was a few years younger than she was now. She wore light khaki pants, which highlighted her muscular legs and her slender waistline, along with a V-neck white t-shirt and a visor. Her luscious brunette locks were just as much Anna Sheridan's as Lola, Christine, Susan, Amanda, and Audrey had.

In the photograph, Willa was luminescent with happiness. Her gaze lifted toward her husband Harvey as she pressed a hand over his chest. If Audrey had to guess, this was the sort of married couple who kept things going romantically. Their love didn't seem stale.

Willa's name wasn't highlighted, which meant that Willa herself didn't have a social media account to speak of. Harvey did, however.

Audrey clicked on Harvey Jackman's name and discovered, to her sincere shock, that the social media company had set up an "In Memory" account for Harvey. His profile picture remained one of him and his wife, Willa, in which Willa pressed a kiss against his cheek and he beamed at the camera. The background was lined with palm trees and glowing white sands. It seemed outside of time.

It seemed incredible that poor Willa had lived such a life prior to her current panicked state. Audrey sensed it would be too much to bring this photograph to the sleeping Willa upstairs. The contrast would be like a bomb.

Beneath the profile picture, many friends and potential relatives had written their condolences for the loss of Harvey.

"He was one of the best guys I ever knew," one friend named Greg Kindel wrote.

"Our community will never be the same," another scribed.

"My heart goes out to Willa. Thankfully, we can rest easy, knowing that he's with Gretchen in heaven."

"Gretchen?" Audrey breathed, curious.

She hurriedly typed "Gretchen Jackman" into a search engine and soon brought up an obituary from twenty years before. There, a photograph of an eight-year-old Gretchen Jackman peered through the screen, immobilized at this age, taken by childhood leukemia. Apparently, Harvey and Willa's creation of the golf outing to "save children from cancer" had been far more personal than the social media post had let on.

"No," Audrey whispered as she stretched a hand over her mouth. Her eyes found Max's sleeping form in his downstairs crib. Unable to control herself, she rushed for him and lifted him against her as a sob escaped her lips.

Being a mother meant being frightened of every conceivable malady, every conceivable accident. It meant being terrified twenty-four hours a day. It meant reckoning with the evils of the world and praying, praying that nothing would befall your babies.

She'd had to live with these fears throughout the entirety of the previous semester. No wonder her grades had suffered. She was biologically programmed to think of nothing else besides this little ball of love.

Back at her computer, she wiped her fingers over her tear-filled eyes and set to work once more, working toward an understanding of Willa's past. She opened a new search for Harvey Jackman and found his obituary.

The obituary began:

Harvey Rhett Jackman left this world on the evening of July 27,

2021, leaving behind his loving wife of thirty-five years, Willa Jack-man, along with a number of lovely friends and coworkers who thought the world of him.

It seemed clear that Harvey's death had something to do with Willa's psychosis. But as Audrey read, she discovered that the obituary offered no cause of death. She clicked out of the obituary and continued to hunt.

Several links down on the main page, Audrey discovered the headline:

POWER PLANT CLAIMS LIFE OF BOSTON SUBURBAN LOCAL

Audrey's heart leaped into her throat. Based on what Willa had said only an hour and a half before, Harvey had worked tirelessly at a power plant, long hours that had clearly worried her. Audrey clicked through to find a horrifically short article, which simply stated that a man named Harvey Jackman had been involved in an electrical misstep at the local Boston suburb power plant, which had resulted in his untimely death. The article also mentioned that Harvey had been a manager at the company and that the company had labeled the accident "user-error."

Audrey's throat tightened at this. User error? This seemed terribly poisonous. A man had lost his life; a woman had lost her husband. In the wake of this, the power plant itself had set themselves up for absolutely zero blame. It didn't sit right with Audrey. She smelled a rat.

Audrey leaned back in her chair and crossed her arms tightly over her chest. Max remained deep in sleep, as did Willa upstairs. Hurriedly, she grabbed her phone, hungry to talk to someone about her discoveries. Her mother, unfortunately, didn't answer after six rings. She then gaped at her phone, confused as another name came to her mind.

She wanted to call Noah about this.

But she knew she shouldn't. Was she out of her mind? It would just complicate things further. Noah was probably wrapped in the arms of that girl she'd seen him with. Probably, they'd picked out little Christmas gifts for one another and had inside jokes and had already begun to tell one another their deepest, darkest secrets. Granted, Audrey and Noah had already done much of that over the summer— but each time Noah had tried to make her his girlfriend, she'd shoved off the topic and said it frightened her to become "exclusive," especially with everything she had on her mind.

She was some kind of fool, wasn't she?

Instead, Audrey puffed out her cheeks and kept searching.

The power plant itself, located on the western edge of a northwestern Boston suburb, was called Greenwich Power Plant. The power plant had begun service thirty-five years ago and had an okay online presence, at least on the surface. In fact, it seemed that recently, they'd hired some kind of out-of-college social media guru to post photographs and update "fans" of the goings-on at the factory. Somehow, this social media person had made the factory seem halfway glamorous if that was even possible. Men in hard hats smiled out happily, as though every day, they longed to wake up and head to the power plant to give their time to society.

Audrey's stomach curdled even more at the sight. She dug deeper, using as many keywords as she could think of. She typed in: Greenwich Power Plant Deaths, Greenwich Power Plant No Safety, and Boston Power Plant Worries... None of these gave any indication that anything was amiss.

Audrey clacked her fingernails across the table as her eyes glazed over. Max cooed, a sound that made her heart jump, but she soon calmed herself down as he shifted his head from side to side and then quieted.

She returned to the "In Memory" page for Harvey Jackman. There, she continued to hunt through the messages from well-wishers. As she scrolled, her mother texted her with a **"Hey honey! Sorry I missed your call. Is everything all right?"**

Audrey continued to scroll without answering. Somehow, some way, she had to find the sentiment that Willa had illustrated during her psychotic episode. She couldn't be the only one who thought the power plant had some sort of vendetta against its workers.

Suddenly, Audrey found it.

A woman named Julia Limperis had written the following:

Greenwich needs to own up to all these deaths.

Audrey's heart leaped into her throat. Beneath the comment, fifteen people had "liked" it, proof that others felt the same. She quickly clicked on this woman's name.

Julia Limperis seemed to be in her forties with a brand-new grand baby and an affinity for home-cooked waffles and reruns of NCIS. But what was her connection to the Greenwich Power Plant? And why had she said this thing about Greenwich owning up to "all these deaths"?

Unlike the majority of other social media users, Julia still had her phone number listed on her account.

Audrey's heart pumped with intrigue. She lifted her phone, wondering if she was actually brave enough to take this next step. Two years before, when she'd taken on her first article for the Penn State newspaper, she'd downloaded an app that allowed her to record the person she spoke to on the phone. This app allowed her to transcribe the interview for the article itself and had proved to be incredibly handy for various musician, artist, or teacher interviews. Audrey had even used the app here and there during her Chicago-based internship— the very place she'd picked up one-half of Max's genes.

But was she actually brave enough to try to get to the bottom of whatever this power plant story was? It was possible that she currently barked up the wrong tree. After all, she'd hardly written anything of any real journalistic integrity. She'd hardly sunken her teeth into anything with real texture. Probably, this semester's grades were proof enough that she should keep a wide berth of this world.

Yet here she was, her phone poised.

And upstairs, Willa was this story's potential victim— under severe psychosis, totally out of her mind. Didn't she owe it to Willa? Didn't she owe it to the rest of the Sheridan family?

Audrey turned on her recording app, dialed the woman's number, and waited for four rings before she answered. When the woman's Bostonian accent rang through the speakers, Audrey nearly dropped her phone to the ground with surprise. People just didn't answer the phone anymore.

"Hello?" the woman asked again, clearly exasperated.

"Hi! Hello." Audrey sounded green as could be. "I'm terribly sorry to bother you like this. But I happen to be related to someone you might be friends with. Someone who befell tragedy at the Greenwich Power Plant."

Julia scoffed. "Which one? Gosh, there have been so many. My poor Randy. So many of his friends..."

"Randy?"

"My husband. Randy," Julia told her.

Audrey's eyes watered with sorrow and fear. "When did Randy pass away?"

"You mean, when did the faulty electricity up at the power plant take my husband away from me? When did those jerks stop paying attention to safety and wind up paying me enough for Randy's funeral to keep my mouth shut? It's been about three years now. Three years. And not a day goes by that I don't think about going to burn that power plant down.

Audrey's eyes widened with surprise. "My god."

"Of course, nobody on God's green earth has ever recommended burning a power plant to the ground for revenge," Julia continued. "So I suppose I have to come up with something else. Granted, it's all in their favor, isn't it?"

"What is?"

"They're dealing with the poorest of the poor. The only times they really have to advertise the deaths is when one of the deaths is upper management."

"You mean, like with Harvey Jackson?"

Julia seemed to smirk into the phone. "They really wish they could take that one back. I'll tell you that."

Audrey's heart lurched. "How many other deaths have they covered up?"

"It's difficult to say. Since my Randy was there, maybe seven or eight? I'm sure there's been more since before Randy. The widows and I mostly keep to ourselves. It's not like getting together to talk about it does anything but remind us of what we've lost."

"But you know who these other widows are?" Audrey demanded.

"Yes, of course. We all know who the others are," Julia returned.

"Would you and the other women that you know be up for being witnesses?" Audrey asked, her voice rasping.

"Witnesses? Why? I don't understand."

"I think this thing deserves a reckoning," Audrey said firmly. "You've been silent for too long."

Chapter Sixteen

Three days later, on December 23rd, the time for frantic pre-Christmas preparations began. There were final Christmas cookies to bake, meals to prep for, gifts to wrap, and final decorations to hang. Around eleven o'clock, as Audrey continued to scramble through another host of transcriptions for her Greenwich Power Plant interviews, something she'd been hard at work at since her earlier findings— a figure, completely obliterated from sight by a stack of glossily wrapped Christmas presents, erupted through the back door of the Sheridan house. The three top boxes teetered as the figure shuffled through, and a gasp of fear rang out. Whoever this wannabe Santa was, she probably wouldn't make it to the Christmas tree.

"You okay?" Audrey leaped up from the dining room table and hustled toward the mudroom just in the nick of time, able to drop down and catch the three top presents as they careened toward the ground.

Susan's face appeared in the space where the presents had

been. She grinned playfully, her cheeks rosy and bright from her walk from the house next door. "Thank goodness you were there, Aud. You saved Christmas."

"Ha." Audrey laughed, turned on her heel, and paraded into the living room, where she placed the presents at the base of the Christmas tree, alongside fifteen or sixteen other presents.

"I see Grandpa Wes has the most presents this year, as usual," Audrey said as she stepped back, assessing the gift tags. "You hear that, Grandpa? You've been good this year!"

Grandpa Wes, who'd gone down for a nap around an hour before, remained silent on the other side of the door.

Susan dropped down to her knees and aligned the presents beautifully, stacking them and pressing them back beneath the Christmas tree limbs with expert precision. Nobody did Christmas like Susan Sheridan.

"Not like any of us need anything," Susan said with a laugh.

"What's that?" Lola appeared at the base of the steps with Max in her arms, her curls bouncing. "You suggesting you didn't get me anything this year, Susie?"

Susan rolled her eyes. "No, Lola. I, of course, got you something. I got all of you something. I couldn't resist."

"That's the spirit of Christmas, Susan," Lola teased. "Annoyance at your own generosity."

"Is that what the Bible says?" Susan asked. She then lifted and tapped Max's plump hand lovingly in greeting. "Hi, there little, Max! How did you sleep?"

Max buzzed his lips and giggled in response. Audrey, overwhelmed with love, stepped forward to take him from her mother. Lola had agreed to babysit for her over the previous few hours, as she'd listened through her interviews, compiled quotes, and transformed the stories into one larger truth about the evils of the Greenwich Power Plant. Audrey was so grateful for her mother's assistance— and it had shed new light on her early years with Lola when she had scrambled through journalism school and then her journalism career, all with little Audrey in tow.

"How's the work going?" Lola asked.

"Not bad," Audrey affirmed, grateful to have Max's weight in her arms again. "I got some really excellent quotes from some of the widows. And two women died as well, one five years ago and one twelve years ago. Their children have given me really great quotes, if heartbreaking."

"It's just so awful what's happened to them," Susan interjected. "No wonder Willa couldn't handle it."

"When do you think you'll have the article finished?" Lola asked.

"I'll have a draft done in a few hours," Audrey told her.

"Ah. A few hours! You're so close. Why don't you get back to work? Max and me are having a grand old time and we wouldn't want to keep his momma away from her journalistic endeavors."

Audrey puffed out her cheeks as her mother took Max back into her arms. Distracted, she dragged her hair into a ponytail and turned her eyes back toward her computer.

"I think it's important that we talk to Willa about what you've discovered sooner rather than later," Susan said softly.

Audrey's throat tightened. "She hasn't had any kind of episode since that afternoon three days ago."

"Yes, but she had been doing so well before that," Susan replied tentatively. "I don't want it to be two steps forward, one step back for the rest of the winter. She's been with us for a few weeks now. We understand more and more of her past and maybe that can help us all create an appropriate future for her."

"Well, she has to stay with us," Lola affirmed. "There's no question about it. She's in no state to be alone or by herself somewhere else."

There was silence for a moment. Susan seemed to ponder Lola's words until Audrey finally interjected.

"She just wants to be with her sister. It was the only thing she really knew when she arrived here. You two and Christine are the closest she can get. Once she's healthy and happy again, I'm sure she'll bring so much love and happiness into our world. She already dotes on Max like she's his great-grandmother. Maybe she kind of is." Audrey fluffed her ponytail, proud of her words. Since she'd taken on this story, she'd felt an internal confidence she'd never found before within herself.

Susan headed back to her place to wrap presents and prep for tomorrow's Christmas Eve dinner. Lola gathered Max's things and headed back to the log cabin in the woods she shared with Tommy, saying that Audrey was welcome there for dinner "any time that night."

"Tommy's with Stan tonight," she said as she settled Max's car seat in the backseat. "And I'll make your favorite. Like old times."

"You mean my favorite from when I was a kid?" Audrey asked, her hands on her hips as Lola placed Max delicately in the car seat. "Macaroni and cheese? Corndogs? What?"

Lola whipped around and gave Audrey a bright-eyed smile. "You'll see. I'll make something that will take us right back to, say, ten years ago."

"Well, gosh. The junk food that came through our house back

then would have made Aunt Susan faint," Audrey said with a laugh.

Lola allowed silence to fold over them. She clicked the seatbelt over Max's carrier and then stepped back, closing the door. When she turned back, her ocean-blue eyes were difficult to read.

"I'm just so proud of you, Aud. Finding this story and diving in head first without any reservations. All from the cozy walls of that house right there." She shook her head. "Honestly, you've grown up so much this year. I hope you know that."

After Lola weaved the car up the gravel driveway and out onto the main road, out of sight, Audrey returned to her stance at the dining room table, her fingers poised over the keyboard. Throughout the previous semester, it had felt like she'd had to pull every article or essay from the insides of her mind with a painful amount of strength.

This article, however— arguably the most important piece she'd ever put together, seemed to write itself.

It read:

The day Margorie Paterson arrived at the Greenwich Power Point to find her colleague, Paula, in a heap on the floor, she knew better than to go to the bosses about it. This was the third death in less than two years, and the upper management of Greenwich Power Plant had made it clear that the body count had nothing at all to do with them.

"It just broke my heart," says Paula, who worked at the plant for nearly ten years. "Knowing that people I loved and cared for at work might not make it through."

Paula, herself, never mentions her own safety, but it was clear that entering the Greenwich Power Plant meant bargaining with one's own life.

Middle-management worker Harvey Jackman lost his life as recently as July 27, 2021. Unfortunately for Greenwich Power Plant, a death in middle management wasn't something they could sweep under the rug. Harvey was a much-loved member of his community. He organized yearly golf fundraisers for children with cancer, as his own daughter, Gretchen, from a previous marriage, died of leukemia.

"People are poor. They need their jobs, and they're afraid to speak out," says one current employee at the Greenwich Power Plant, who has asked to remain anonymous. *"Harvey's death was a huge tragedy, but so were all the others. It's time for action. No one else should lose their lives."*

Audrey typed into the late afternoon and early evening, at which time she read and re-read, edited and re-edited the piece, printed it out in her mother's printer, and then headed off to Lola and Tommy's cabin with her heart stuck in her throat.

If this article did what she needed it to do, they would find justice for Harvey and Willa and others who'd lost their lives in the tragedies. They would potentially investigate new regulations at the power plant itself, thus breaking the never-ending cycle of deaths.

Finally, Audrey felt she upheld that quote within the frame her mother had hung on her wall.

"Journalism can never be silent: that is its greatest virtue and its greatest fault. It must speak, and speak immediately, while the echoes of wonder, the claims of triumph, and the signs of horror are still in the air," she said the words to herself as she sped toward the cabin.

Lola had decorated the cabin with minimal Christmas decorations. Audrey had to guess that Tommy wasn't the sort who wanted to go full-hog on things like garlands and bulbs, and Lola edged on the "lazy" side when it came to all of that, anyway. When Audrey had been a little girl, they'd often just set up a miniature Christmas tree and decorated it with little pieces of wrapped-up chocolate and a tiny, glowing star on top.

"Look, Aud! I told you. I made your favorite from ten years ago." Lola lifted a baking tray from the oven and grinned wildly, showing off a big batch of melted cheese- and veggie-laden nachos.

"Oh my gosh!" Audrey smacked a gloved hand over her mouth as memories washed over her.

"It was our go-to snack there for a while," Lola said, placing the baking tray on the stovetop.

Audrey entered her laptop and the printed-out article on the table, stepped toward Max's crib, where he slept like a little doll, then headed straight for the stovetop with all the excitement of the ten-year-old girl she'd once been. She lifted a chip high, bringing with it a long string of melted cheese and several blocks of black olives and green peppers.

"I had a hunch you didn't bother to eat much while you worked on that article," Lola said, beaming. "That's how I always am when I fall into something the way you have. Everything else plays second fiddle."

Lola sat at the table with a plate of nachos beside her. There, she flicked through Audrey's print-out, reading with incredible focus. All the while, Audrey paced distractedly, unable to eat any more of the nachos until her mother finished and gave her assessment.

The last thing Audrey needed was for her mother to tell her

how much of a failure she was, too. She just wouldn't be able to handle that.

But when Lola lifted her eyes toward Audrey's, they were wide with wonder. She rapped her red pen across the center of the last page and said, "Audrey, you really have something here."

Audrey's lips parted with surprise. "You think so?"

"It's better than most of the other garbage I read in our Boston newspaper," Lola told her. "And probably better than anything I could cook up at age twenty."

"Don't say that!" Audrey placed her hands on her hips as her heart performed backflips across her diaphragm.

Lola flung her arms out on either side of her and said, "Audrey. I'm going to send this to my editor."

"Really?" Audrey demanded.

"Absolutely. It's a top scoop and dammit—" Lola's eyes shifted with sorrow. "I hope this enacts real change in that community."

Audrey returned to her ravenous nacho-eating, stuffing herself silly with relief. Lola used this time to highlight several passages that she felt needed to be tightened. "But that's just standard in the world of journalism. Nothing you should worry yourself about," she explained. "And you know? I think you should email this to your professors in the journalism school. Not sure they're always reading the Boston newspapers all the way over there."

Audrey dropped her cheese-laden chip to her plate and gaped at her mother. All the color drained from Lola's face.

"Audrey? What's up? You look like... Oh my god. What happened?"

"Mom... This semester almost destroyed me," Audrey breathed, her voice wavering. "I missed Max so much. I missed the

Vineyard. I felt tugged between so many different realities. And then, I accidentally slept through my alarm for my last final, which meant I ended the semester with a 2.52-grade point average. That's not high enough to stay in journalism school."

Lola's expression grew stoic. After a long pause, she asked, "That's it?"

Audrey laughed outright. "What do you mean?"

Lola shrugged and lifted the printed-out article. "I don't know, hon. I don't really care if you slept through some silly essay-driven final exam. You can write the daylights out of most other students in journalism school. I think you're going to be just fine, no matter what happens next. Penn State should beg you to come back. But you know just as well as I that there are no straight paths forward in life. Maybe you don't need a traditional four-year school diploma to dictate what you should do. Maybe you need something else. Whatever it is, we'll find it together. Deal?"

Audrey's eyes welled with tears of relief. "It's a deal, Mom."

Chapter Seventeen

T hat evening, Lola, Audrey, and Max drove back to Susan and Scott's place to speak with Willa. On the way, Lola called Willa's new psychiatrist, a woman named Sheena Collins, to ask her to be present. Sheena, who'd seen first-hand the confusing hurricane Willa's head had been over the previous weeks, agreed whole-heartedly, asking that they meet in Susan's driveway beforehand to allow her to catch up to speed.

Sheena Collins looked to be in her late forties with thick, horn-rimmed glasses and curly, short hair. Her coat seemed three times too big for her, like a sleeping bag she could carry around with her everywhere. When she leaped into the back of Lola's car to greet them, her tone was confident yet gentle, something you wanted to hang onto during the darkest times.

Audrey launched into what she had recently learned about Willa's situation back in her Boston suburban community and her belief that the loss of her husband contributed to Willa's break with reality. Sheena listened intently, taking notes and asking appropriate questions when needed.

"Is it appropriate to just tell our Aunt Willa what the reality is?" Lola asked as her brows furrowed. "Or will it confuse her too much?"

"The trouble I've had with Willa thus far is there was no real understanding of the past forty-five years of her life. She left the island as a young child, and she returned as an adult. The gap was so sinister, and she couldn't help us fill it." Sheena's eyes latched onto Audrey's. "It seems like you've found a way to at least lead her mind to that gap, stare into it, and start to understand what went wrong. As devastating as it might be for her, it's absolutely necessary to get to the next stage of her mental health journey."

Max coughed himself awake there beside Sheena in the backseat. Sheena's eyes widened in sudden fear as Audrey scrambled out of the vehicle and then back in to lift Max out of his seat. It was funny seeing this woman several years older than Audrey, with all the education in the world, to not know what to do about a baby's presence.

As Sheena slipped out of the car, she admitted it. "My sister has a toddler as well, and I must admit that I feel ill-equipped. The way she handles him and speaks to him and sings little songs with him... It's a funny thing. I spend my days with some of the sickest people on the island. And then my nephew tries to get me to sing, 'Row, Row, Row Your Boat,' and I'm at a complete loss."

Audrey bobbed Max against her little frame gently and gave Sheena a warm smile. "I never pictured myself as a mother, either. It just kind of happened. And now, I guess, the little things become so natural. I'll be singing 'Row, Row, Row Your Boat' in no time."

Sheena nodded firmly and toyed with the engagement ring on her right finger, something Audrey hadn't noticed previously. It was a strange thing to think about the enormous backdrop of a psychiatrist's life— their own problems, their own fears.

"If I didn't know any better, I would think my fiancé hired you to say that," Sheena teased quietly. "It's funny all the things we're afraid of in life, isn't it? And yet, time happens to us regardless." She gestured up toward Susan's house, where Willa unknowingly awaited them. "Let's help Willa. You can see it in her face, what kindness and love she has within her. I can't imagine what evil people created this world for her. She never deserved it."

They found Willa at the kitchen counter with Kellan, her mouth half-filled with uncooked cookie dough and a big wooden spoon in hand. Her stirring was powerful, seasoned, and her laughter was filled with joy as Kellan flipped through modern radio stations, showing off his favorite R&B songs and pumping his head in time.

"This kid is teaching me how to be hip," Willa told the others. After a moment, however, her eyes found Sheena's, and the corners of her lips curved downward. "Hi, Sheena," she greeted timidly as she placed the wooden spoon against the side of the mixing bowl. "If you wait just three minutes, we'll have fresh cookies."

Susan's footsteps sounded from the top of the circular staircase. In a moment, she appeared, her brunette locks swept back behind the shoulders of her cream-colored turtleneck. "Hi there," she greeted them. "Shall we sit in the dining room?"

A few minutes later, the oven beeper sounded. There was the gentle tap of the baking tray as Willa placed it on the stovetop. The sinful smell of Christmas cookies, freshly baked, rushed from the kitchen doorway. Audrey placed Max delicately back in his carrier and splayed her curls behind her ears in anticipation.

When Willa appeared in the doorway of the dining room, she held a large platter of just-baked cookies. Audrey could envision this same woman performing just this action, time and time again, throughout her days as a stepmother to Harvey's daughter, who'd died, and then as a beautiful and devoted wife, one who'd longed to create a marriage just as prosperous and loving as her parents' marriage had been deceitful and dark.

We're all trying to fight against our instincts, Audrey thought then. But sometimes, time drags us under.

Sheena used what seemed to be clinical, psychiatric-approved language to begin the proceedings.

"We understand that you've had a difficult time since your arrival to the Vineyard," she began. "As we discussed in our meetings, you've entered a state of psychosis, which, at your age, is ordinarily brought on by some sort of trauma. When we attempted to dig into your memories, your mind resisted."

Willa nodded as her eyes glistened.

"Do you want to know what happened to you?" Sheena asked. Her voice was gentle and coaxing.

Willa closed her eyes tightly and inhaled deeply. "I think it's the only way through," she admitted finally. "I feel like there's this great big crater where my heart should be."

Audrey passed Sheena the envelope she'd brought to her mother's, in which she had placed several photos of Harvey Jackman from the internet, including the one from the golf outing and the vacation he'd taken with Willa during happier years.

Before Sheena showed Willa the photographs, she said, "You've been involved in a tragedy, Willa. A real tragedy that shouldn't have befallen anyone, and certainly not a woman as kind and loving as you. I'm going to say a name to you. And I want you to know that as you understand this name and understand what happened, we're here for you. The medicine is working within you. Soon, clarity will give you a fresh start. Okay?"

Willa's smile waned still more. Her skin was the color of crepe paper.

"About thirty-five years ago, you married a man named Harvey Jackman," Sheena said as she slid the photograph from their beach vacation toward Willa.

Willa's lips parted with shock. Her eyes glowed with tears as she lifted the photograph to eye level and seemed to gaze directly into Harvey Jackman's eyes.

"My God..." Willa shook her head ever-so-slightly, her face lined with disbelief. "Harvey..."

It didn't take long for the truth to fling out from the back alleys of Willa's mind. The next half-hour was a flurry of words, stories told and told again as Willa described the events that had led up to and proceeded after Harvey's death at the plant.

"I told him I didn't want him working there any longer," she started to explain, her words staccato. "But he said we only had a year left till his retirement when we could do whatever the heck we wanted. I'd already retired from my work within the school system, as there had been cut-backs and they just didn't have space for me up there any longer. This meant that all I did, every damn day, was go on my walks, read my books, and worry myself to death about Harvey's safety up at that godforsaken power plant. And then one day, I got the phone call saying there had been an accident.

"Naturally, the power plant immediately said that the accident was Harvey's fault." Willa closed her eyes against the pain of it all as tears cascaded down her cheeks. "I spoke with a lawyer around then, but things were quite foggy after that. Even around the funeral, I had to step into a side room to deal with these penetrating thoughts. I couldn't figure out where I was when I stepped out of the side room. Someone had to put me to bed. Someone suggested I'd just drank too much."

Audrey's heart swelled with sorrow. She reached across the table and placed her hand delicately over Willa's. Willa made no motion to move it. "That Greenwich Power Plant seems to have been the site of many, many deaths over the years— even ones that they attempted to cover up," she began.

Willa's eyes were hollow with this news. "I told him not to go back there," she recited.

Audrey glanced back toward her mother, who shook her head delicately. Perhaps talk of a lawsuit belonged to another day. Today was about the emotional toll of losing someone you loved with your whole heart and mind— someone you'd tied your story to for thirty-five years until ultimately, disaster meant you had no story any longer.

"How are you feeling, Willa?" Sheena asked after a couple of minutes of silence.

Willa gestured around her temple and exhaled. "I still have these strange thoughts stirring. It seems like my brain wants to shove this knowledge to the side again and live in the reality I created for myself."

"That will happen," Sheen affirmed. "It's a natural thing that your mind wants to protect you."

"I'm going to fight it," Willa breathed. "I want to stay in this reality. I want to hold Harvey close to my heart with my memories.

It feels like ages since my brain knew his name. Yet here it's been the whole time."

"The mind is a funny thing," Sheena told her. "It can play terrible tricks on us. And there's sometimes no telling why. In fact, it's estimated that scientists only understand how about ten percent of the brain works. That gives us a whole lot of room for error."

Willa puffed out her cheeks and glanced toward Audrey once more. "How did you learn about all of this?"

"It was something you said," Audrey whispered. "It made me start digging."

Willa's eyes shone with tears. She then directed their attention to the photograph of the golf outing, where Harvey Jackman beamed with life and vitality. "He was so pleased this day. We raised two hundred thousand dollars to fight children's cancer. Gosh, when we lost his little girl... It tore us both up inside, but Harvey was never the same after that."

"I had no idea you had a stepdaughter," Susan lamented, her eyes heavy. Only just that year, she herself had become a stepmother, something she'd probably never thought she'd ever become. Life threw many curveballs, that was for sure.

"I loved her to bits," Willa breathed. "We had such a unique friendship, just the two of us. When I was first dating and figuring out what I wanted my life to be, I told everyone that I didn't want children. I remember it so clearly now. I thought for sure that I would turn out just like my mother." Willa closed her eyes against the heaviness of this sorrow. "But when Gretchen looked at me, she gave me all the love in the world. And it made me consider for the first time that maybe, I didn't have to be like my mother. Maybe I'd never been like her. Maybe, in some small way, I'd always been more like Anna. Filled with love and hope for whatever future I could bring."

A few moments later, Willa admitted that she was exhausted and wanted space and time to think alone. She thanked the Sheridan girls and Sheena for this safe passage back to the truth, then stood on quivering legs and headed for the guest bedroom. After the door clicked closed behind her, Lola, Susan, Sheena, and Audrey sat with bated breath. Max kicked his little feet in his carrier, seemingly sensing the tension in the air above him.

"It's going to be a long road," Sheena breathed. "But this was one of the first steps forward."

"Thank you for your help," Susan said hurriedly. "I can't imagine how that might have gone without a trained professional."

"It's really nothing," Sheena replied. "If you have any other problems over the next few days, please don't hesitate to call me. Willa and I have another appointment right after Christmas. We'll go through more mechanisms together so that she can train her brain not to go into that dark place again."

As Sheena gathered her coat, gloves, and hat, Susan's phone began to buzz on the countertop in the kitchen. She hustled to go grab it, leaving Audrey and Lola alone in the dining room. Audrey exhaled all the oxygen from her lungs and gazed up at the mistletoe in the far corner of the dining room, which, hilariously, Kellan had noticeably avoided like the plague since Susan had hung it up.

"You did a good thing today, kid," Lola complimented. "Finding the story and naming the truth is never an easy thing. But this was especially difficult. It has links to my mother, Anna. It's lined with a horrible family tragedy."

"Sometimes, I ask myself how anyone has the strength to keep going," Audrey replied then. "When I found out that I'd basically failed the semester, I walked around with stones in my stomach for days. I felt like such a failure. What happens when— when real tragedy happens?"

Lola's eyes filled with tears as she laced her fingers through Audrey's over the tabletop. Audrey could feel the pain behind Lola's eyes— could practically feel the eleven-year-old version of her, who'd lost her mother to a boat accident and then Susan later that year, who'd abandoned the island due to the fear and darkness within her own heart.

"Tragedy comes for all of us," Lola whispered. "But some of us are damn lucky to have a whole lot of love in-between."

Susan appeared, suddenly breathless, in the dining room doorway. She pressed the phone against her chest as her eyes widened.

"Christine's at the hospital," she stuttered. "It's real this time."

"Oh my God! Oh my God!" Lola erupted from the dining room table and sprung for her coat.

"Max! Do you hear that?" Audrey cried. "We're getting a brand-new cousin! And just in time for Christmas Eve!"

Chapter Eighteen

The contractions had come, powerful and strong and only five minutes apart, mid-way through Christine and Zach's now-annual viewing of *It's a Wonderful Life,* which seemed only fitting given that the whole movie was about the risks you take in life to build worlds for the ones you love. Christine groaned at the powerful, minute-long contraction as it rolled over her belly, tightening it and moving to her lower back, then billowing across her stomach once again. Zach's eyes were wide with fear when he turned his head her way, a Dorito poised near his lips.

"Is this it?" he asked, his voice hardly a rasp.

"This is it, baby. This is it."

Zach sprung into action after that. He hustled to the bedroom, where he collected their overnight bags, then raced into the kitchen to lodge upwards of thirty Christmas cookies into Tupperware containers, calling out, "If your entire family is up there, which they're bound to be, then I reckon we have to feed them with something."

Christine puffed out her cheeks as her thoughts ducked into a back alley of her mind. Her hands stretched out on either side of her rotund stomach as she came to terms with reality: at the end of this painful tunnel, she would be a mother. After years of turmoil, of bad dates, of worse relationships and of heartache and loss— she would finally fulfill something she'd always thought was reserved for others and not herself.

Zach reappeared in the living room with the overnight bags flung over one shoulder and a stack of Tupperware that towered from his chest to his chin.

"Are you okay, honey?" Zach asked.

Christine lifted her chin so that her eyes met his. "This time, I'm really and truly ready."

Zach grinned ear to ear, even as his eyes shimmered with fear. "Let's get you up there."

True to form, Lola, Susan, Audrey, Baby Max, and Amanda were already at the hospital upon Christine's arrival. When Christine was settled into her room for the next hours of labor, Lola and Susan stepped into the brightly-lit, overly-white room with excited smiles.

"Oh. What are you doing here?" Lola asked Zach, teasing him. "I thought this was sister's only?"

Zach rolled his eyes and turned himself toward the doorway. "I'll head out and grab myself a cup of coffee. Give you girls some space." He then pointed playfully at Lola and said, "But there's no contest between us today, Auntie. I'll be in that delivery room, whether you like it or not."

Lola and Susan burst into laughter as Zach disappeared into the hallway. Lola collected Christine's hand in hers as Christine rolled through another contraction, squeezing Lola's fingers into a twisted mess. Lola, to her credit, said nothing until the contraction was over.

"You're a strong one, Christine Sheridan," she said. "Have you considered weight lifting in the Olympics?"

"Yeah, right," Christine returned as she burrowed her head back on the pillow. "How long are these things supposed to last, anyway?"

"What? Labor and delivery?" Susan asked, erupting with laughter.

Christine dotted beads of sweat from her forehead. "I always read different accounts. Some people are like, 'My baby just came out!' And other people are like, 'I was in labor for forty-eight hours and then just gave up and decided to have a C-section.'"

Lola and Susan giggled as Susan grabbed a handkerchief from her purse and wiped Christine's forehead for her.

"Don't worry about the time, Chris," Susan said gently. "We'll be up here till that baby decides to show him or herself. We'll even push Christmas back if we have to."

"Gosh, that's right," Christine breathed. "A Christmas Eve baby."

"Gosh, your baby will have some stuff to say about that," Lola teased playfully. "Combined birthday and Christmas presents." She clucked her tongue. "I can't imagine a worse life."

Three and a half minutes after the first, another contraction rolled through Christine. After, she gasped for breath as Susan grabbed her a cup of water. She then settled back, closed her eyes and said, "I'm just so grateful to have you two here with me while this happens."

"Where on earth would we be otherwise?" Lola asked with a little laugh.

"Come on, Lola," Christine said pointedly. "We spent most of our years apart. I never thought in a million years that I would settle down on the Vineyard, fall in love, and have a baby. I never thought in a million years I would have the kind of happiness I saw other people having. I know that having that happiness means making a daily choice to remain happy. I know you have to work for it. But I'm so, so glad to have you two by my side so that we can continue to choose that happiness together."

Susan blinked back tears as Lola let out a sob, which she soon suppressed.

"Look at you. You aren't even a mother yet, and you're getting so sappy," Lola stated.

"Stop that," Susan scolded her.

"We love you, Christine," Lola offered finally, her voice cracking. "I don't know where my life was headed before Susan dragged us back to this island, but I know it wasn't a terrific place. It certainly wasn't here at the hospital room on December 23rd, waiting for my brand-new niece or nephew to be born."

Christine closed her eyes as another contraction rolled through her. Even as the intensity of them mounted, they seemed to mentally get easier, as she registered, with each passing moment, that each contraction got her closer to meeting one of the great loves of her life.

After the contraction finished, Susan assured her she was "Doing great." Lola, being Lola, asked, "So, what can we expect here? Boy or girl?"

Christine rolled her eyes playfully, grateful to have Lola to keep her mind off the pain. "Do you have any requests?"

"Oh. I didn't realize you were taking requests!" Lola cried. She then lifted her eyes toward Susan. "What do you think, Susan?

We've got all kinds of nieces. And your son doesn't seem to come to the Vineyard enough to make any real impact."

Susan crossed and uncrossed her arms. "He has a family of his own. You know that."

"Yeah, yeah. I know that," Lola said playfully. "But we're just talking logistics here. I think we might want to press Christine for a little boy?"

Susan rolled her eyes. "I refuse to play this game. I'll love whatever baby Christine has."

Christine and Lola burst into laughter. For a split-second, it was as though they were just little kids again, with Susan lording over with her "big sister" power. Perhaps some things never truly changed.

Zach returned to the hospital room a little more than thirty minutes after Lola and Susan's arrival. He sipped a second cup of coffee and admitted that he'd gotten into a silly conversation with Audrey and Amanda, who argued about who was cuter— Ryan Reynolds or Ryan Gosling.

"Oh gosh. That's a tough one," Lola affirmed. "Which side did you come out on?"

"Well, I have to admit, I'm a Gosling guy," Zach replied with a wink.

"I bet Audrey's a Gosling girl," Lola returned.

"You'd be right about that," Zach said.

"And Amanda's all Reynolds, all day," Christine piped up.

"How did you know?" Zach said with a vibrant smile.

"He seems like her type," Christine said.

"Do we know if she's made it official with our gorgeous front-desk manager?" Lola asked, turning her head up toward Susan.

Susan exhaled. "She's pretty guarded about the details. I hate it. I want to ask her every day."

"She's doing everything on her own time," Christine said tenderly. "At forty-three and delivering my first baby, I think I'm in line to understand that."

The hours stretched on as the contractions grew more powerful, more urgent. Christine found herself sometimes able to laugh, to joke, to be herself, while other times, her mind raced off elsewhere as she languished in her pain.

Sometime after midnight, Audrey became the figure at Christine's bedside while the others took breaks in the waiting room. There was a lightness to her that Christine hadn't recognized since summertime, and her laughter came easily, beautifully, as Christine made some joke or another, like, "Look, now it's me in the labor position instead of you. Pretty crazy, huh."

"I wouldn't trade you, that's for sure," Audrey teased right back. "But it sounds like it won't be long now. You're doing so well— much better than me."

"I don't know about that, Audrey. You seem to have something figured out that the rest of us didn't get around to till we were much, much older," Christine said softly. "I hope my baby knows you as well as I've gotten to know you."

"I promise you this, Aunt Christine. Me, you, Max, and your baby will always have a special bond. We can even form a little club. We'll hang out at ballet recitals or soccer matches, or school plays. We'll be the two head honchos of the PTA club. We'll be the model mothers who make all the best snacks for the field trips. Everyone will hate us. But we won't care."

Christine closed her eyes as her laughter mixed with a hiss of pain. "I like what you're saying, Aud," she said finally. "I have to admit; it's a relief not having to go through this new motherhood thing alone."

Audrey's eyes grew shadowed. The clock on the wall ticked toward one in the morning, which put Christine at around four and a half hours thus far in the hospital room. Christine wasn't sure if it was a nightmare or another dimension or the greatest adventure on earth.

"I've decided to stay on the island for the foreseeable future, by the way," Audrey confessed. "I just can't be away from my baby another night. It's too hard. But really, Christine. I can't thank you enough for all you've done. I'm sure you have such a wonderful relationship with Max now. Something I'll never really understand."

Christine shook her head somberly, recognizing how difficult this all was for Audrey. "Max is such a wonderful baby. It's been a pleasure to help raise him. But in the grand scheme of things, I had him for only around three and a half months, if that. That's just a blip in a little baby's life. Just a small chapter in what will be a beautiful story about you and your son."

Audrey swallowed and dropped her eyes to the ground. "Thank you for saying that," she whispered. "I love you very much, Christine. And I'm so grateful that beyond our relationship as aunt and niece... We get to be friends, too."

"Some of the best of friends," Christine agreed.

The door creaked open to allow Zach to poke his head in. His eyes seemed frenetic from all his coffee-drinking, but his smile was sure and confident. "Mind if I steal Christine for a while, Aud?"

Audrey slipped back out to allow Zach to step into his position as partner and father, there at the side of the bed. He linked his fingers with Christine's and lifted it to kiss the top of her palm delicately.

"I just walked up and down those hallways, giving Audrey the time she wanted, thinking the same thing over and over again," Zach said softly.

"And what's that?"

"I just can't believe I get another shot at happiness," Zach continued. "I can't believe I get to love you and our baby. The love seems almost too big like my heart might break."

"I feel the same right now," Christine breathed. "A huge amount of love, plus this huge desire to get this delivery over with already. I wish there was a way to communicate with the baby that we're ready."

Zach laughed good-naturedly as he adjusted on the chair beside the bed. "You know, I've been thinking about this next year. How it sounds like it'll just be you and me and baby at the house, now that Audrey plans to stay on the Vineyard for the foreseeable future."

Christine nodded, unsure of where he headed with this.

"I think we should set a date for our wedding, Christine," Zach continued, his voice catching. "I've loved you for a year and a half. And I know that love will only blossom and flourish."

Christine closed her eyes as her heart swelled with longing.

"Say something," Zach said.

Christine's smile felt electric. "I just have to make sure I lose the baby weight before I shove myself into the wedding dress of my dreams."

Zach laughed outright. "Come on, Christine. I would marry you in this hospital gown. I would marry you with nothing on at all."

"Wow. I guess we'd have to talk to my wedding-planner cousin Charlotte about a potential nudist wedding. It's never been done on the Vineyard," Christine joked.

"Christine!" Zach cried playfully, rolling his eyes. "Just say you'll marry me this summer. When the Vineyard skies are impossibly blue, and we can spend the whole day along the water, celebrating our love."

Christine's eyes welled with tears, even as the beginnings of another contraction took hold of her.

"I'll marry you, Zach. This summer," she whispered. "I promise you."

Chapter Nineteen

Christine gave birth to a healthy baby girl on Christmas Eve morning at 9:45 am. Audrey, who'd eventually had to collapse back at home with little Max, received the news via a phone call from her mother, who'd paraded on through the night, armed with "many cups of coffee and, admittedly, a few sips from Tommy's flask."

"How does she look?" Audrey asked, yawning as she pressed the phone against her cheek and poured herself an additional cup of coffee.

"Mom and baby look amazing," Lola affirmed. "Christine was a real champ. Zach, of course, had a few moments of weakness, but that's just men for you."

Audrey laughed appreciatively. "He looked on the verge of tears all night last night."

"He's an emotional one. But I think we like that in the Sheridan clan, don't we?" Lola asked with a laugh.

"Any name yet?" Audrey asked.

"Nope. I think Susan and I might head out of here soon to give Christine, Zach, and baby some space. Susan's exhausted and keeps snapping at me that there are a million things to get done before Christmas.' I guess the whole Montgomery-Sheridan gathering is still on for tomorrow?"

"I wouldn't have wanted Christmas any other way," Audrey replied.

Grandpa Wes and Kellan appeared in the mudroom, kicking their boots of mud and discussing some wilderness-themed poetry, which Wes had apparently gotten Kellan into.

"That's the thing about Wordsworth," Kellan said excitedly. "He's so visceral when he talks about the way the wind moves through the trees and the water rushes across the stones."

"That's exactly why I like it, too," Wes affirmed as he stepped down the hallway. "He takes you there immediately. You don't even have to step outside, and you feel this breath of fresh air."

Audrey lifted Max against her and greeted Wes and Kellan with a bright smile.

"Guess what! Christine had a healthy baby just about an hour ago," she announced.

Grandpa Wes dropped his red cap to the ground in surprise. He then smacked a hand across Kellan's shoulder and said, "How about that!"

Kellan laughed good-naturedly as he slid out from beneath Grandpa Wes's over-powered grip.

"Boy or girl?" Wes asked.

"A girl," Audrey replied brightly. "Gosh, I'm jealous. Christine will get to pick out all these little dresses and hats."

Max buzzed his lips playfully as his blue eyes glowed up at her. Audrey immediately regretted her words.

"No, no, Max. I don't mean it," she told him. "I just wish boys had more interesting clothes, is all. I wouldn't trade you in for the world."

A few minutes later, Scott and Willa arrived at the Sheridan house. Willa was bundled up in a thick periwinkle winter coat and a black cap, her hands shoved in her pockets. Her eyes were tinged pink, as though she'd spent a good deal of the previous twenty-four hours crying. Scott said that he had to run some pre-Christmas errands, all from a mile-long list that Susan had written out for him, and suggested that Willa and Audrey hang for a while. Scott's words hung in the air, a reminder that nobody wanted Willa to be alone for too long.

"Of course," Audrey said brightly. "Come on in, Willa."

With Scott and Kellan off to run errands and Grandpa Wes alone in his room, Audrey and Willa sat across from one another at the kitchen table wordlessly, both waiting for the other to chime in. Audrey felt strangely guilty, suddenly, for bringing to light what had happened to Willa. Perhaps it had been a blessing, for a little while, not to remember the immensity of her loss.

"I called several people from our hometown last night," Willa said suddenly, surprising Audrey with the strength of her voice.

"Oh..." Audrey's eyes widened.

"Yes. Some of the widows of men who'd lost their lives at the plant, along with several of my friends. People I hadn't thought about since before all this chaos in my head started. Some of them had been very worried about me. Others had heard that I'd gone to visit family. I finally traced the root of this rumor. Apparently, after my psychosis had begun, I told a close friend, Rhonda, that I was headed to visit my sister. I suppose that's why they didn't send out a search party. That, and there's something about a sad widow. Something people don't want to get too close to, I suppose."

"It sounds like those people love you a great deal," Audrey countered. "I'm sure it was really good to hear from you."

"I didn't tell everyone what happened," Willa offered. "But I did ask a closer one advice on what to do next. Lola has been very vocal that there's space for me here on the island. Perhaps it's time to return to that chapter of my life and allow it to flourish this time."

Audrey's throat tightened. "I can't speak for everyone else in my family. But I can say this. We were broken for years. And now that we're back together, we're stronger than ever. I know what your parents did to you probably messed you up forever. Add to that Gretchen's death from leukemia and Harvey's death... It's really no question why your mind went a little haywire for a while."

Audrey reached across the table and gripped Willa's hand. "All those memories you have with Anna. Maybe you could help us create new ones. I have my son and Christine just had a daughter. I know they'd love to have another member of the family to love. And give them Christmas and birthday gifts, of course, but mostly, the love thing."

Willa erupted with natural yet surprised laughter. "I think you're right about that. Perhaps it's time to look hard at building a life here on the Vineyard. Family is the most important thing of all. That's what I've heard, anyway. And it would be good not to be in that house where Harvey and I... Well. We loved one another to bits. It was never perfect. Maybe nothing ever is, but my heart knows he was my first and only true love. How grateful I am to have had him as long as I did."

That night, Audrey, Amanda, Willa, Max, Kellan, Susan, and Scott gathered around the television at the Sheridan house and watched, *It's a Wonderful Life*, which they'd heard was the film Christine and Zach had been in the midst of when Christine had decided it was time to head up to the hospital to have her baby girl.

Audrey placed her head on her grandfather's shoulder as Max slept in the corner in his little carrier, his blue eyes moving slightly behind his thin eyelids, searching for something in his dreams. On the screen, Jimmy Stewart sang, "Buffalo gals, won't you come out tonight?" to a beautiful young woman and skipped down a black-and-white sidewalk in an impossibly different era. One day soon, Jimmy would make this woman his wife.

"I just can't believe it," Grandpa Wes said, heaving a sigh.

"What's that?" Audrey whispered as she reached into the bowl of pretzels and popcorn on the couch-side table.

"I can't believe I have a brand-new granddaughter," Wes replied. "I don't know what I did to deserve all this goodness at once."

Audrey's grin widened. She nibbled at the edge of a popcorn kernel as Susan pressed her finger to her lips to shush Wes, as she wanted to focus on the film she'd probably seen at least fifteen times, maybe more. Audrey and Grandpa Wes exchanged silly glances, both wanting to burst into childish giggles about Susan's reaction. Susan wouldn't have been able to handle that.

After the movie, Susan said, "Good night," to everyone and announced that Christmas celebrations began at the Sunrise Cove Inn at ten-thirty a.m. sharp. "We'll have a little breakfast buffet set up followed by a full-scale Christmas dinner around four-thirty," she said.

"With plenty of cookies to sustain us between breakfast and dinner, I guess?" Audrey teased.

"The number of cookies that have been baked..." Kellan said as he shook his head with disbelief.

"Let's just say we haven't been able to use our kitchen for a while," Scott stated, jabbing Susan gently with his elbow.

After that, Willa, Susan, Kellan, and Scott embarked through the frozen edge between the Sheridan house and the Frampton house, leaving Audrey, Amanda, Max, and Grandpa Wes alone.

"I'll see you girls in the morning," Grandpa Wes said as he snuck his arms over his head and erupted with a yawn.

"Love you, Grandpa!" both Amanda and Audrey called as he escaped into his bedroom.

Amanda then collapsed on the couch and wrapped her hair into a tight ponytail, her face pinched.

"What's wrong, honey?" Audrey asked her, using a Susan tone.

Amanda seemed not to notice the fake-Susan-mode. "Sam asked me to be his girlfriend. Like, officially."

"And?"

Amanda's eyes were dark, fearful. "I mean, I don't know."

"What do you mean, you don't know? Sam's your world. Not to say that you can't have your own opinion. You very clearly can. I just think... why not Sam?" Audrey asked tenderly.

Amanda buzzed her lips distractedly. "I know. And honestly, Audrey, I love him. I realized it even in the silence after he asked me. But I get so worried. Chris really messed me up. I thought for sure that would be my reality. My future..."

Audrey dropped her chin to her chest. "I suppose all we know for sure is that nothing is for sure. And we have to go with our gut, sometimes. As we've seen with Willa, and with our grandmother, and with our mothers themselves... things change, fast as lightning. The moment is here-and-now. That's what's most important."

"The here-and-now," Amanda whispered. "How about that?"

"How about it," Audrey countered playfully.

Just then, as though God himself had a hand in how the night would play out, Audrey received a text message.

"Are you going to get that?" Amanda asked after the buzz.

Audrey lifted her phone, read the word "NOAH," and immediately flung the phone to the other end of the couch. Her heart beat as quickly as a rabbit's.

"What the heck was that?" Amanda asked.

Audrey's eyes widened. "I don't know."

"You mean that you're not following the here-and-now, knocking on your door demanding that you pay attention to the advice you just gave me," Amanda teased.

Audrey heaved a sigh, lurched up, and grabbed her phone. She knew that if she didn't read it for many hours, she would toss and turn with fear and resentment. It was better to face it head-on.

NOAH: Hi. Merry Christmas Eve. Through the grapevine, I learned that Christine had a healthy baby girl. Congratulations to all of you.

NOAH: I'm sorry things were so strange when we saw each other on the street. I didn't even know you were back. I'm sorry if I didn't respond correctly. I'm sorry I didn't handle it well... I'm just sorry, all around.

NOAH: I would really like to talk to you before you head back to Penn State. Maybe we could grab a coffee.

"Oh my gosh. Why won't you tell me what's up!" Amanda

flailed a pillow against Audrey's thigh as silence swelled between them.

Audrey lifted her chin to blink at Amanda, gobsmacked. "It's Noah," she finally said.

"You're kidding."

"I'm not."

"He's so sad right now! It's Christmas Eve, and he misses his Audrey!" Amanda cried.

"Oh, stop it," Audrey insisted.

"I will not stop it."

"He wants to see me," Audrey said.

"And...? Will you see him?"

Audrey squeezed her eyes closed. A million little memories rushed through her mind— the first meeting at the vending machine at the NICU, the movie dates and the beach outings, the time he'd held her tightly as they'd careened through the waves on a dramatic sailing expedition— it had all mattered to her. And it had brewed up something within her that very much seemed like love.

"I think I have to," Audrey breathed.

She finally lifted her phone once more and typed back.

AUDREY: Merry Christmas Eve to you, too.

AUDREY: I'm not going back to Penn State. It's a long story.

AUDREY: But... Noah. I'm so glad to hear from you.

AUDREY: And I'd like to see you soon, too.

Chapter Twenty

Grey-black smoke billowed out from the Sunrise Cove Bistro's kitchen as a fire alarm blared on high. Susan bolted out of the swinging door, her hair a wild frizz. Still more smoke streamed out the door, all from the back oven, following after Susan as if its life depended on her. Upon the stovetop, two burnt pies sat, crisp and black.

"Gosh darn it," Susan muttered as she headed for the supply closet.

"I got it, Aunt Susie," Audrey called. She reached the closet before her aunt, grabbed the stepladder, and then headed for the little square of hardwood beneath the fire alarm. In a flash, she made her way up the ladder then hit the fire alarm, which stopped the horrendous wave of beeping. She then cackled as she stepped back, saying, "I know you love that sound, Aunt Susan, but I think we should stick to Christmas tunes from now on."

Susan blushed as she strung her hair into a high ponytail,

which she immediately dropped back down. "I don't know what got into our normal cook. Having a baby one day before the big family Christmas celebration..."

Scott jumped out of the kitchen, as did Lola and Tommy, who seemed in the midst of preparing a semi-disastrous holiday meal for the entirety of the Sheridan and Montgomery families. Max waved toward Lola, his grandmother, from the carrier near the door, and Lola all-but melted at the sight.

"Oh gosh, Audrey, you put him in that little Christmas sweater I got him," Lola cried as she rushed toward him.

"Stop right there, Missy," Susan belted. "We have two Christmas meals to finish. It's only nine-forty-five in the morning, which means we have forty-five minutes more to get our act together. There will be no cuddling our grandchildren until after success."

Lola stuck out her tongue at her older sister as Audrey stepped back toward Max, waving her hands through the air. Obviously, the text from her Aunt Susan saying, "Come around whenever you want!" had been a kind of trap.

"Audrey, I have things for you to do if you can spare the time," Susan said firmly.

There was no choice. Once the kitchen was cleared of smoke, Audrey propped up Max's carrier in Zach's back office, rolled up her sleeves, scrubbed her hands, and set to work on slicing enough fruit and vegetables to feed a small army. Bright red radishes, juicy peppers, plump strawberries, and little Christmas pears soon lined the Christmas-themed platters. All the while, Lola, Tommy, and Scott worked diligently, knowing that Susan would use all manner of manipulation to make them work faster if they didn't already do it themselves.

By ten-forty-five, miraculously, the Christmas buffet was set-up, fresh pies were in the oven, and the Montgomery and Sheridan families had begun to stream in, all wearing ridiculously bright smiles, greeting one another with hugs and kisses and big, glossily-wrapped presents, talking overly-so about the weather and how much snow they'd gotten that year, and generally setting themselves up for the all-day present-giving and eating-drinking event there at the Sunrise Cove Inn.

Audrey put Max down for a nap in the next room and then changed into a maroon-colored velvet dress with a high neckline and little golden buttons at the cuffs. When she stepped out into the foyer of the Sunrise Cove, she nearly ran head-long into her mother, who wore something very similar— a lower V-cut maroon dress with golden buttons up the center. Audrey's jaw dropped open at the sight.

"You're kidding," Audrey said.

Lola laughed, her hand stretching out across her stomach. "I'm sorry. I didn't realize there was a dress code to this event."

"I didn't realize you wanted to copy your twenty-year-old daughter's fashion!" Audrey cried back.

Lola's cheeks glowed bright red. It already seemed she'd snuck a glass of wine or two, perhaps during Susan's forced labor session. "Honey, don't pretend for a second you didn't get all your fashion sense from me."

Audrey rolled her eyes into the back of her head and then shoved back any sign of embarrassment. It was actually a blessing to be compared to her mother in so many different ways.

"There she is," Lola said as Audrey stepped into her arms for a hug. "My smart, talented, beautiful, cherished..."

"Mom..." Audrey warned her, teasing.

"All right. Is Max all set to sleep the day away?"

"Seems like it," Audrey replied as she turned back to catch the last glimpse of him. "I have the baby monitor right here," she beckoned to the little white device in her purse. "And... have you heard from Christine?"

Lola teetered her head right, then left. "Christine is sad to miss the party, but she's glad she won't be bringing her brand-new baby to a big Sheridan-Montgomery party. Nobody would be able to resist holding her. All those germs."

"I understand," Audrey affirmed, remembering her first few days with her own baby and feeling at such a loss that she hadn't been able to hold him, as he'd been terribly sick.

"I told her we'll be thinking about her non-stop over there," Lola said softly. "To think it's her first Christmas as a mother." Her eyes then widened as she added, "Heck, it's your first Christmas as a mother, too, isn't it?"

Audrey laughed. "Pretty crazy, huh? So much has happened. It feels like way more time has passed and that Max should be a teenager or something."

"Don't say that," Lola warned. "Because it really does happen just like that." She snapped her fingers. Lola's face steadied once more as she added, "By the way. My editor loved the piece."

Audrey's heartbeat sped up. "Oh?"

"He wants to publish it later this week. I told him your pay rate was forty-five cents per word."

Audrey's jaw dropped with surprise. "Forty-five?"

"That's nothing later on, when you become a truly sought-after journalist," Lola told her, her voice low. "You need to remember to ask for what you're worth. In all things. Work, relationships, family matters. Everything."

Audrey knew to keep these words to heart.

Just after, Audrey and Lola stepped out in nearly-matching dresses and found themselves in the midst of a chaotic Sheridan-Montgomery Christmas Family Reunion. The Bistro featured three large Christmas trees; the limbs of each were heavy with bulbs and tinsel and little hanging figurines. Each tree was topped with a large angel figurine. The angel figurines were turned out toward the rest of the large room, where a large buffet table had been set up near the broad window, which allowed for a beautiful view of the surging Vineyard Sound outside. The buffet table was lined with the promised Christmas Buffet— complete with scones, muffins, pancakes, scrambled eggs, a wide selection of cheeses, fruits, sausages, both patty and link, along with mimosas, Bloody Marys, and a number of different juices.

Susan stood near the door to greet everyone, her smile infectious. Nobody could have guessed that only an hour before, she'd nearly set the kitchen on fire.

"Audrey!" Claire's sixteen-year-old twins, Gail and Abby, rushed up to greet Audrey, who they'd fallen for over the previous two summers. Audrey offered wit, charm, and enough irony to allow the two red-headed teenagers a bit of perspective when it came to things like boys and high school. Their cousin, Rachel, who was Charlotte's daughter, bucked up behind them, grinning wildly to show a bit of frosting on her lip.

"Hi, girls!" Audrey cried, hugging each of them briefly.

"Where is Max?" Gail asked.

"He's resting. He doesn't have any obligation to hang out with family until he can walk and talk," Audrey explained, which resulted in the three teenagers nearly falling over with laughter.

Audrey had never had extended family as a teenager. If she had to guess, based on what her friends had told her back in Boston, having forced hang-outs with family members as a teenager was a terrible fate. Audrey wished she could tell them how much they should appreciate these moments with loved ones but knew it was too earnest. Jokes were better. They would learn the rest themselves, anyway.

The next hour or so became a flurry of Christmas morning activity. Audrey felt tossed between the teenagers, to Rachel's mother, Charlotte, who spoke about a recent wedding ceremony she'd arranged for yet another celebrity, to Andy and his new wife, Beth, who seemed basically as enamored with one another as teenagers on their way to the high school prom.

"They should really bottle whatever it is you have," Audrey teased them.

Beth laughed wildly and stretched her hand across her stomach. It was rumored that Beth was pregnant, although she and Andy hadn't given this fact out to the Sheridans quite yet. Even still, Beth glowed with a powerful aura, one that very much resembled the one Audrey had when she was pregnant.

Audrey escaped back to the buffet table to pour herself a mimosa and watch the crowd from the corner. Off to the left, Willa told a joke to Aunt Kerry, who regarded her with a mix of curiosity and excitement. By this time, everyone in the Montgomery-Sheridan clan and probably a whole lot of Martha's Vineyard community had learned about Willa's presence on the island. Just looking at her now, however, Audrey could only perceive a gorgeous and high-spirited woman, one who felt on the brink of building a brand-new life with people who already held her dear, if only because of her forever-connection to Anna Sheridan.

Off to the right, Grandpa Wes and Uncle Trevor seemed deep in a nostalgic conversation, one that buzzed with, "No, I'm pretty sure that was 1978, not 1979, although we also had a big football championship in 1976, so maybe that's what you're thinking of..." — the kind of thing that made Audrey shake her head and smile. The texture of Wes and Trevor's friendship was insurmountable. Audrey prayed to have that with the people around her later.

Perhaps that texture would come with Gail, Abby, Rachel, and Amanda, as they were all around her age, with a high probability of staying on the island.

Her heart prayed, at least, that they planned to stay on the island. Her heart prayed that some of these people around here would be around her thirty years from now. Her heart prayed for the beautiful longevity of the family.

Suddenly, her phone buzzed in her purse. She lifted it to find a text message from none other than Christine.

CHRISTINE: Hey. I hate to miss today.

CHRISTINE: It wouldn't be Christmas without you.

CHRISTINE: Would you mind having a little FaceTime call? I would love for you to meet my daughter.

Audrey nearly leaped from her skin. She placed her half-drunk mimosa on the buffet table and hustled for the door, feeling half-frantic.

"Where's she going in such a rush?" someone asked someone else. "And did you notice that she and her mother are wearing the same dress?"

Audrey couldn't have cared less. Once in the foyer, she found herself still in the midst of the Sheridans and Montgomerys, who seemed to spill out from every dimension. No privacy, especially on Christmas. She ducked down a long hallway, then sought refuge near the washing and drying machines that lined the back supply closet. Above the machines hung an old photograph of Wes Sheridan alongside his father, Robert— an iconic islander and a man Audrey would never know. Here, in this strange supply closet, Audrey would meet the next great love of her life, Christine's daughter. It was a strange mix of feelings.

Audrey dialed Christine as her heart hummed in her throat. After a long moment, Christine's beautiful face glowed out of her screen.

"Look at you!" Audrey cried.

Christine laughed. "You don't have to lay it on thick. I know, I still look exhausted. I think I'll look exhausted the rest of my life."

"Don't be silly. You look stunning."

Audrey's eyes welled with tears as Christine moved the phone back slightly to show Zach, who held the teeniest little burrito-wrapped baby in his strong arms. The shadows beneath Zach's eyes were thick, yet his smile was stellar.

"Hi there," Audrey said. "There's the new dad."

Zach looked on the verge of tears. Probably, he'd spend the next eighteen years like that— just painfully in love and willing to cry about it.

"We miss you, Audrey," Zach said.

There was then a trade-off, as Christine placed the phone on the bedside table and took the little girl in her arms. Zach then held the phone to allow a full view of mother and baby. Audrey wanted to make a joke about Zach's camera skills, but soon forgot all about it as she took in the sight before her. Christine slowly lifted the sides of the swaddle to allow Audrey to see her gorgeous, porcelain-skinned baby, with translucent eyelids and the tiniest little fingers, all cramped up against her stomach as though she held onto something that she planned to hide from her mother for as long as she could.

"My gosh, Christine," Audrey whispered. "My gosh."

"I know." Christine's nostrils flared with wonder. She lifted her eyes back toward Audrey's, and they held one another's gaze.

"And we just named her," Christine finally added, her voice breaking.

"Oh!" Audrey cried.

Audrey's eyes widened. "Oh!"

Christine's grin widened. "I know. It's not customary to wait so long. But we're not exactly customary parents. And we wanted to see what fit her."

"I think that makes all the sense in the world," Audrey whispered. She hurriedly swiped away a tear, then asked, "What's her name?"

"Mia," Christine said softly. "Mia Audrey Walters."

Audrey's lips parted with surprise. "Mia Audrey?"

"We had to include you in our family, the way you've included us in yours," Christine explained.

Audrey sat watching the beautiful Mia Audrey Walters sleep for the next few seconds as her heart swam with love and expectation for the years ahead. Probably, Audrey would know all there was to know about Mia Audrey. From first steps to first words to first bicycle rides— she yearned to know every menial moment in this little girl's life. She even yearned to buy her a few outfits, which was a perfect loophole in the whole "having a baby son" issue.

"I think you three are about to have the greatest adventure," Audrey whispered, knowing that she had to head back to the Sheridan-Montgomery Christmas. "And I can't wait to be a part of it."

"Good to have you back, honey," Christine said. "We missed you so."

Back in the Bistro, Audrey continued to enjoy the beautiful mid-day Christmas celebration. Grandpa Wes had his glass of wine raised and a fork against the edge, dinging it to alert everyone that, as was tradition these days, he wanted to say a few words.

"Merry Christmas, everyone," he announced in his deep baritone voice as the crowd settled down around him. "It's difficult to begin this speech, mostly because, well, once I get started, I don't ever want to stop."

Several people in the crowd chuckled at that, including Audrey. She then hustled around behind her grandfather to grab her mimosa, which made several people in the crowd laugh harder.

"Oh, that's just my granddaughter," Grandpa Wes teased. "She's a new mother these days— another beautiful blessing upon the Sheridan family, and for that reason, I guess she needs to have her fun while she can." He winked at Audrey as she slid past, her mimosa in hand.

"And besides that, the blessings that have been brought this year have been boundless," Wes continued. "Just yesterday, my middle daughter, Christine, had her first baby. I think right now, she and her husband are in the midst of trying to figure out what to call their daughter. But I'm certain they'll call me when they get that worked out."

Audrey's smile widened as she felt the heaviness of this beautiful secret. Mia Audrey. Her cousin.

"Besides that, my eldest daughter, Susan, married the love of her life. Scott, it's been such a pleasure to welcome you officially to the family." Wes lifted a glass toward Scott, who held onto Susan with both arms wrapped around her waist lovingly. "With Scott, I've welcomed a brand-new friend and step-grandson, if you can believe it. Kellan, you've opened my mind in ways I never could have imagined. And you've forced me out of the house when I least wanted to. I can't thank you enough." Kellan lifted his soda back toward Grandpa Wes lovingly.

The speech went on, with mentions of Andy and his new bride, Beth, along with Kelli's recent sale of the iconic Aquinnah Cliffside Overlook Hotel, which had once belonged to Robert and Marilyn Sheridan, Wes and Kerry's parents.

"The minute we walk through the halls of that beautiful hotel, I know we'll feel mother and father with us again," Wes said, his eyes shining with tears. "And it's all thanks to you, Kelli. And you, Xavier. Thank you for bringing this vision to life." Grandpa Wes lifted a glass to Xavier, who had purchased the property and allowed Kelli's recently-found blueprints for the old place to be the mission of the redesign. It was truly a spectacular thing.

As Grandpa Wes's speech ran on, Max's little squeal erupted through the baby monitor. Audrey hustled back through the crowd, her mimosa in hand, and then slipped back into the side room to find her ten-month-old vibrant, his little legs kicking wildly.

"There you are. Did you think you were missing everything?" Audrey said as she dropped to her knees before him.

Audrey lifted Max into her arms and then sat on the ground, her legs crossed and Max cradled against her. For a long moment, Max was comforted only from the warmth of her body and leaned heavily against her, calm and quiet. In the next room, Grandpa Wes's voice was a soft, pleasant lull.

In the quiet of herself in this tiny closet-sized room, Audrey gave thanks for all she had — for Christine and Mia Audrey, for Willa and her mother, for Grandpa Wes and even Kellan. Her heart felt squeezed with love. She felt it might break.

Chapter Twenty-One

Audrey's article appeared in *The Boston Globe* on December 27th. By December 28th, the article itself had gone viral on social media and had been shared upwards of three hundred and fifty thousand times. Apparently, the article had struck a nerve with the United States populous, as it outlined ideas of workers' rights and incompatible working conditions. Multiple workers from multiple factors across the States had begun to organize worker's strikes in order to demand better working conditions and accountability.

It felt as though Audrey had struck a match— and now, the rest of the United States would help that fire burn.

Audrey wore only an old t-shirt and a pair of boxer shorts. Her computer was open before her so that she could read tweets while she fed Max the baby food she'd whizzed through the Vita-mix for him. He dabbed his lips over it excitedly and squawked at Audrey, as though he sensed just how happy she was. Probably, he did.

@mandymoralous tweeted: @audreysheridan finally said

what needed to be said. Workers, unite! It's high time we stand up to people who look at us like we're less than human.

@hunderson tweeted: @audreysheridan you are the GOAT. You're why I want to go into journalism. You're changing lives.

Audrey's eyes widened as she continued to read. Due to the lack of concentration, she accidentally got a bit of pea-smash on Max's cheek, which resulted in him giggling wildly.

"Oh, sorry, bud," she said as she smeared a rag over his cheek.

Suddenly, the back door pushed open to bring Christine and baby Mia in from the chill. Christine walked delicately, still unsure about her body, and soon collapsed at the kitchen table with Audrey and Max.

"You're out of the house!" Audrey cried as she jumped up to wrap her arms around Christine.

"Barely," Christine replied. "This place is basically an extension of my house."

"Where's Zach?"

"He's sleeping," Christine returned as she set Mia's baby carrier down between their chairs. "Poor guy tired himself out taking care of Mia. He let me sleep deep into the morning, though. Bless his heart. Guess we'll be missing each other for a few months while we both pick up the slack." Christine shook her head as her face illuminated. "Funny that such a tiny, tiny thing would take up so much worry and time."

"And then they grow into monsters," Audrey said as she gestured to Max, who smacked a plastic spoon across his highchair and giggled.

Christine laughed. "Hi, Max. I miss having you around, you

know."

Max beamed at her knowingly, as though he fully acknowledged that he and Christine had had their time together and that time was now complete.

"So..." Christine's eyes shimmered. "How about this article?"

Audrey grimaced. "It's been a whirlwind. I've gotten so many tweets and emails. Another newspaper wants to do a follow-up and include some of my quotes. Another newspaper wants to interview me on how I got the scoop. I won't do anything like that. I feel like it's invasive of Willa's story."

"That makes sense," Christine agreed. "But no doubt, you did a good thing with this article. I just read a tweet that said the Greenwich Power Plant is closed until further notice so that state officials can investigate what went wrong."

"Oh gosh. I didn't even see that," Audrey said, her eyes widening.

"Journalism can do excellent things," Christine said softly. "And so can you."

Audrey's shoulders dropped forward. "I guess Mom told you that I had to drop out of college...again."

"And this entire Greenwich Power Plant story is proof enough that that's okay," Christine offered. "Everyone has to find their own way. Me. You. Max. Mia. We're all just going through life, making it up as we go along."

"And what has Mia made up so far?" Audrey asked, her smile widening.

"Good question," Christine offered. "She's still trying to figure out what she likes, exactly. Right now, she's more of a fan of the left breast rather than the right."

Audrey winced. "Breastfeeding is a whole other battle. I was sad, though, when we had to wean him off so early when I headed back to college. I think it's a really intimate, really important time to bond with your child."

"I've talked with mothers who like both ways," Christine said. "And I don't want to shame myself one way or the other. But right now... I have to admit; it's a trial. And it's all thanks to my little finicky daughter, who seems to know what she wants."

Audrey laughed appreciatively, despite knowing that behind these words were sleepless nights and, probably, Christine's anger toward herself. It would eventually fade. Other feelings would transplant it. But this was the here and now of having a brand-new baby and it wasn't easy, but then again, motherhood was never easy.

Just then, Audrey's phone dinged with a new email.

"Are you going check that, rock star journalist?" Christine asked.

Audrey grumbled and lifted her phone to find an email from none other than Ms. Evans, her previous journalism counselor.

Audrey,

I just finished reading your piece in The Globe. I know I speak for the rest of the journalism staff here at Penn State when I say — WOW.

I know it's been difficult for you, having a new baby and attempting to take on such a huge course load.

And I know I said that we couldn't welcome you into the journalism school any longer. But in light of your recent article, we would like to make an exception and welcome you back to Penn State this semester. You have real talent, Audrey. We hope to help you hone that talent.

Ms. Evans

Audrey read the email allowed to a rapt Christine. After a long pause, Christine and Audrey both burst into laughter so loud that Max blinked at them, confused.

"Yeah, right," Audrey said finally.

"It sounds like when a boyfriend breaks up with you and then wants you back when he hears that you've moved on without him," Christine pointed out.

"Oh my gosh! Yes. That's exactly it," Audrey replied. She pondered the email again, remembering the depths of despair she'd fallen into upon learning that she'd been kicked out.

It had been a whirlwind of a few weeks.

"What are you going to do?" Christine asked.

"I'm not going to respond right now," Audrey said as she returned her attention to Max's pea-mash. "I'm still basking in the glow of this viral article. And your baby. And all the good things that have come with returning to the Vineyard. I'm not sure I ever want to go back to Pennsylvania."

"You sound like you've made your mind up," Christine noted.

Audrey shrugged. "Do you ever think about what you left behind in New York City?"

Christine furrowed her brow and then turned her gaze back to her sleeping angel, whose little pink cap curled toward her perfect little nose.

"I think about that version of Christine with love," Christine murmured. "I think about how sad she was and how she tried to cover up that sadness with alcohol or men. And I wish I could tell her... Gosh. I wish I could tell her that there's another way. But

193

back then, I saw nothing except the life I had. Everyone around me did the same thing all the dang time and then one day, Susan and Lola called me back here. And I realized just how empty that all was.

"I don't say these things for any kind of pity," Christine offered then. "I say them to suggest that, well... One day, you might look back at that semester at Penn State and realize it didn't matter at all— none of it did. It just got you to where you are now, is all."

Audrey's throat tightened at the thought. "Do you think the pain ever gets you anywhere?"

Christine pondered this for a moment. "I think it makes us sit in the silence of ourselves and ask ourselves what we actually need to survive. But I'm not sure it 'gets us' anywhere. I don't think it's a currency. And I do think it's up to the ones we love to help us carry the burden of that pain."

Audrey held the silence for a moment as she pondered the weight of what Christine had just suggested. Just then, however, her phone buzzed— and she lifted it to find a message from none other than Noah.

NOAH: I happened to read a pretty spectacular article from a now world-renowned journalist.

NOAH: If you're actually still around the Vineyard, I would love to catch up.

NOAH: Just let me know when you're free. I'm not up to much.

Audrey's eyes widened as she flashed the phone around for Christine to read. Christine blinked tired eyes toward the message, read it, and then gaped with excitement.

"You should go," she said suddenly.

"What? No."

"Come on. I'm not doing anything today. I can watch Max and Mia all at once," Christine coaxed her. "Trust me. Like I said, Zach let me catch an extra hour's sleep today. I feel like Superwoman."

"You're sure..." Audrey's eyebrows lowered with distrust. Suddenly, she flung herself into a standing position and headed toward the staircase, saying, "Oh my God. I need this so badly, Aunt Christine. I need to feel like I'm twenty years old again. Or else I might explode."

While Christine waited downstairs for Audrey to change into her date clothes, the back door screeched open to reveal the beautiful Willa, who stopped short in the doorway between the mudroom and the rest of the house, her smile flourishing. "I had no idea you'd be here," Willa said, as though Christine, Max, and baby Mia's presence enchanted her.

"Hi, Willa! Merry Christmas," Christine greeted. She rose up to hug the older woman, again feeling that strange stab in her gut — a reminder that Willa was the closest she would ever get to Anna Sheridan. It was both painful and beautiful, all at once.

Willa stepped toward little Mia and gazed down lovingly, clearly rapt with the tiny human. "She's really beautiful, Christine," Willa breathed. "I can hardly believe it."

Christine knew that Willa had struggled a great deal— that she'd decided not to be a mother due to her problems with her own mother and that she'd lost her stepdaughter to leukemia. Still, she'd longed for a child and perhaps regretted her decision, just a little bit. It was difficult not to. Christine had regretted hers before her surprise pregnancy, too.

Willa's eyes watered as she slipped into the chair alongside Christine, still captivated with Mia. "It's been such a whirlwind since the article came out," she told Christine. "People are reaching out to me left and right from Harvey and I's hometown. I've also met with Sheena, my psychiatrist, twice to handle the fall-out from all this."

"How are you feeling?" Christine asked softly.

Willa met her gaze for a moment. "Surprisingly lucid. Surprisingly good. But beyond anything, I feel..." Willa's lips quivered. "I feel loved in a way I haven't since Harvey passed. It's different, of course. But the love within the Sheridan and Montgomery family is like a firmly-built house. It's shelter from that wild storm we call life. I suppose it's a blessing, then, that my psyche pointed me in this direction on the hunt for Anna. I'd like to think that Anna herself came down and led me this way. Who's to say, though."

"I don't know about you, Willa. But I believe in angels," Christine whispered, her heart lifting into her throat. "And maybe what you're saying is right. Maybe my mother saw your pain, your suffering. Maybe she saw Susan's and Lola's and my suffering, as well. Maybe all of us being here on the Vineyard together is some great scheme of the angels and God himself. I can't speak for them. I can only speak for the amount of love we both feel here in the Vineyard. It's spectacular."

Willa reached across the table to grip Christine's hand. Just then, Audrey swept down the stairs, a vision in the same magenta gown she'd worn for Christmas Day. Her hair curled wildly down her back and shoulders, and her eyes were lined with charcoal, giving her a mysterious and sultry look.

"Where are you off to?" Willa asked, her voice light, as though she'd asked Audrey Sheridan the same question time and time again.

"I think she's about to go tell someone she's in love with them," Christine said sneakily. "I'm not totally sure, though."

Audrey's cheeks burned red with embarrassment. She swung her coat across her shoulders, then approached to plant a kiss on Max's cheek.

"I hope you two don't spend all night at this table gossiping about me," Audrey said. "I'm sure there are plenty of other interesting things you could do to pass the time."

Willa erupted with laughter as Christine crossed and uncrossed her arms over her chest, her smile waning.

"You look beautiful, honey," Christine said finally, slicing through the anxious humor Audrey had created. "I hope you know that wherever you go, and whatever you do, you'll have that light with you, always. I love you. We all do."

Audrey paused at the doorway to the mudroom, her hand poised over the crown molding. Her eyes watered with gladness as she pondered what to say next. But before she could, a horn blared out from the driveway— proof that Noah had come to pick her up.

"I love you, too," Audrey breathed.

In a moment, there was the rush of the back door as Audrey sped out into the night. In the silence that followed, it was just Christine, her newborn baby, baby Max, Willa, and the twinkling Christmas tree. She knew, in a flash, this moment would be gone. She prayed to hold onto it as long as she could.

Coming Next in the Vineyard Sunset Series

YOU CAN NOW PRE-ORDER A VINEYARD BLIZZARD

Other Books by Katie

The Vineyard Sunset Series

Secrets of Mackinac Island Series

Sisters of Edgartown Series

A Katama Bay Series

A Mount Desert Island Series

Connect with Katie Winters

BookBub: www.bookbub.com/authors/katie-winters
Amazon: www.amazon.com/Katie-Winters/e/B08B1S7BBN
Facebook: www.facebook.com/authorkatiewinters/
Newsletter: www.subscribepage.com/kwsiguppage

To receive exclusive updates from Katie Winters please sign up to be on her Newsletter!

www.subscribepage.com/kwsiguppage

Made in United States
North Haven, CT
20 May 2022

19358548R00114